Finding the Last HUNGRY HEART

Finding the Last HUNGRY HEART

A Novel in Verse by David K. Leff

4/26/21

Kathy,

It's out there waiting to be found!

with affection,
David

PUBLISHED BY HOMEBOUND PUBLICATIONS

Copyright © 2014 by David K. Leff. All Rights Reserved. Without limiting the rights under copyright reserved above, no part of this publication may be reproduced, stored in or introduced into a retrieval system or transmitted in any means (electronic, mechanical, photocopying, recording or otherwise) without the prior written permission of both the copyright owner and publisher except for brief quotations embodied in critical articles and reviews.

For bulk ordering information or permissions write:
Homebound Publications, PO Box 1442
Pawcatuck, Connecticut 06379 United States of America
Visit us at: www.homeboundpublications.com

FIRST EDITION
ISBN: 978-1-938846-23-6 (pbk)

BOOK DESIGN
Front Cover Image: © Hofhauser (Shutterstock.com)
Back Cover Images. (From Left to right):

Image one: Vietnam War protestors march at the Pentagon in Washington, D.C. on October 21, 1967. Source: Lyndon B. Johnson Library. Author: Frank Wolfe

Image two: Trade ad for Grateful Dead's album American Beauty. December 1970 Source: Billboard, page 9, 5 December 1970. Author: Warner Bros. Records

Image three: "Further" / "Furthur", Ken Kesey and the Merry Pranksters' famous bus, Hempfest 2010, Myrtle Edwards Park, Seattle, Washington, 2010, at which time it had recently been restored. Date: August 2010. Photo by Joe Mabel

Cover and Interior Design: Leslie M. Browning

Library of Congress Cataloging-in-Publication Data

Leff, David K.
  Finding the last hungry heart : a novel in verse / David K. Leff. — First edition.
    pages cm
  ISBN 978-1-938846-23-6 (pbk.)
  1. Teenagers—Fiction. 2. Nineteen sixties Fiction. 3. Novels in verse. I. Title.
  PS3612.E34968F57 2014
  813'.6—dc23
                                                                        2013049709

10 9 8 7 6 5 4 3 2 1

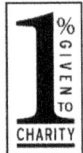

Homebound Publications holds a fervor for environmental conservation. We are ever-mindful of our "carbon footprint". Our books are printed on paper with chain of custody certification from the Forest Stewardship Council, Sustainable Forestry Initiative, and the Programme for the Endorsement of Forest Certification. This ensures that, in every step of the process, from the tree to the reader's hands, that the paper our books are printed on has come from sustainably managed forests. Furthermore, each year Homebound Publications donates 1% of our annual income to an ecological or humanitarian charity. To learn more about this year's charity visit www.homeboundpublications.com.

For all who were there,
Whether you remember or not.

Lay down your money and you play your part
Everybody's got a hungry heart
—Bruce Springsteen, *Hungry Heart*

And kept his heart secret to the end
From all the picklocks of biographers.
—Stephen Vincent Benet, *John Brown's Body*

What is the key word today? Disposable.
The more you can throw away the more it's beautiful.
—Arthur Miller, *The Price*

KING OF THE HILL

Go ahead, call me Dumpster Dempster! Most folks
do, though to my face it's Caleb or Mr. Dempster.
I'm king of a hill called Mount Trashmore,
my kingdom a landfill, one of Connecticut's last
after dumps filled when forbidden to burn day and night
with smoky fires condemning what's used-up and broken.
Now it's compact and cover daily with soil,
shape the mountain's shoulders
to a summit so rain sheds without percolating
to poisonous leachate. Thirty years guarding this gate
for Westmoreland town, now my time is limited
by the mound's geometry, the slope packer trucks
can climb fully loaded. Soon our leavings will find distant
transfer stations, turned to ash and steam in furnaces
of resources recovery extinguishing memory.

I know every soul in this small place
where most drive weekly to my domain, recalling names
and addresses as well as any politician. I knew
their parents, remember how their children
performed in class. Paid to watch that recyclables
are separate from putrescibles, that leaves are composted
and a household's hazardous chemicals are kept away,
I know that Mrs. Westbrook, retired and reclusive widowed

schoolteacher, like a soap opera stereotype, loads peach
brandy bottles into the glass bin each week,
that middle-aged bachelor Josh Root, a welder
and part-time potato farmer subscribes to men's magazines
bundled between copies of *Time* and tossed into the paper
crate. By frozen and fast food containers and discarded
clothing I see relationships broken down
or begun. By signature bags and boxes from stores,
I read who is doing well and who has hit the skids,
who is eating lobster and who is ordering pizza
or letting food rot in the fridge. I know who has bought a new
computer or changes their own crankcase oil.

Confidently I read such offscourings like the ancients divining
by animal entrails. Truck beds and car trunks are steel bowels
clogged with consumed and depleted leftovers
of living—spoiled food, plastic wrappings, broken toys,
cracked ceramics, blackened sparkplugs, and uncountable
cups from endless yesterdays of coffee. I envision
the bulging plastic bags like coins or sticks of an ersatz
I Ching, sure I can read a person's heart by what's spilled
from split sides and burst fasteners. But sometimes a smile,
offhand garden chat, kids' soccer scores, handshake,
or weather small-talk hides suspicions,
resentments, and envies, burning invisible
and unquenchable like an underground landfill fire slowly
eating away years of accumulated leavings. Suckered
by faith in the worthless and spoiled, the end
came up too quickly in the rearview.

Working from a battered Airstream trailer with a desk,
squeaking chair and piles of flyers reciting the rules,
I'm outdoors more than a farmer, pushing, crushing
and back-blading with a bulldozer, or checking
windshield stickers, chipping brush, sweeping
up, using a rake and pike pole to dislodge
a bag or old broomstick caught in the compacter.
I have time and place to sense subtle changes in the sky,

feel seasons turn by odors and the consistency of trash-strewn
ground. I find turtles, muskrats and frogs in the hill's swampy
margins where no one treads, and the top is a stopover
for migrating birds, some exciting ornithologists
with binoculars and spotting scopes, like last year's snowy
Iceland gull. Garbage brings seasonal rhythms with wrapping
papers, leaves, attic gleanings and desiccated garden plants.
By degrees this rising mesa of waste becomes my Walden
Pond by which a world's depth and height is measured.

Joyful garbage!
Frank smells, orphaned existences, abundant universality
and individuality! Steward of a cultural burial mound
like a minor pharaoh's pyramid, I build
a monument for the future, sculpting the landscape,
a time capsule. If New York's Freshkills is visible from space
E.T. explorers will find me too, and if archeologists
reconstruct entire civilizations from shell middens,
pottery shards, bones, buttons, and clay tobacco pipes
I offer worlds of treasures. Newspapers
forty years buried are as readable as the morning
they landed on a doorstep. By our trash I know
we are known, for what we leave lives afterward.

TRASHMORE

Lord of the realm, my word is law
   on this sprawling twenty-two acres fenced with rusting chain
   link and surrounded by cattail swamp where redwings sing
in early spring a gurgling konk-la-ree awakening
me at dawn to an uneven plateau ranged upon by giant diesel
dump trucks and dinosaur dozer tracks at a bulge and bend
of the Seven Mile River where fishers cast into riffles
and pocket water on a stream almost too deep to wade across.

Posted at the gate, my commandments are hand painted red
letters on a white sheet of warped plywood.
Rubbish to the compacter and newspaper to the big dumpster.
Magazines and mixed paper have their bins
as do glass and plastic, but no black. Televisions
and computers fill boxes in a forty-foot steel cargo container
while oil and anti-freeze are funneled each into its tank.
Brush to the chipper, leaves on the compost pile,
construction debris into the roll-off while air conditioners
or a fridge cost more for their Freon. Save hazardous
for a special day when moonsuited attendants
will gingerly grasp paint thinners and pesticides,
prepared to test unlabeled containers. Come elections,
politicians stand and shake hands
by the gray dander piled at the ash pit.

Such a goof for a college anarchist,
but a landfill teaches that time tempers
all things with happenstance and necessity.
Besides, I'm protecting the planet, the sheriff of refuse.
And I don't just live for the dump, but at the dump
in an old fishing camp renovated with discarded junk,
part of the deal when the town purchased
this riverside gravel pit years ago. Vertical board-and-batten
siding cover my cabin, the steep roof for decades patched
with more colors than Joseph's coat, my front door tall
and wide, carved mahogany from a demolished
Victorian mansion, my chimney and fireplace
stone cobbles retrieved from the river.
Living here is part of my pay,
cheap digs traded for round the clock security.

A large garden keeps me in squash and potatoes, cukes,
cabbage, beefsteak tomatoes, zucchini, strawberries, parsnips,
kale and carrots much of the year while sugar maples
along the road and out back drip sap for February's sweet
first crop boiled in a swayback tool shed leaning south.
Living off the land, a hermit at the center of things, my stove,
cabinets, sofa, books, blankets, glasses, dishes and pots
are rescued castoffs and misfits once sentenced
to burial. Out my wavy, prismatically bubbled old windows
lies a mountain with a water view, just what everyone dreams,
what everyone says they want. And I dreamed unwarily
on, until the corrosive itch of politics and private malignancy
transformed my oasis of waste to a nightmare mirage.

DEMPSTER

A UConn degree in history, the dump
gig started part time summers, continuing when college grads
went begging to bang nails or bus tables.
At five foot ten, skin and bones, my high school yearbook
called me "lanky" alongside a photo
showing a crew cut and forced
smile. Now I've a slight paunch and scoliosis
stoop, thinning hair mostly gray tied
to a pony tail below a balding crown and thick brushy beard.

Back in the day of smudgy fires Billy Bartley, second
selectman's brother, scion of a founding family, ran the fill
and charged what he wanted, ruling with 250 plus
pounds, a booming voice and political hook
until collapsing one hot, humid August day into a freshly
dumped pile, his arteries clogged with years of free fish cakes
and French fries from the Third Base Diner
whose driver never paid a dime to dump.

Longest employed among part time students and retirees,
I was acting overseer as months of political wrangling
delayed a decision after I discovered that Bartley
had pocketed thousands in scrap metal receipts.
Nominations blocked and votes deadlocked, I got kudos

for running a clean dump and book learning
that would help with tangles of new regulations.
Besides, I was born in town to high school
sweethearts, my dad a dropout handyman, handsome
with a big smile and a glad hand, my mother
a nurse, nurturing but always in charge.

Money good and a place to live, I took the job
for want of what else. Here I could find myself famous
long ago, grounded on my own total loss farm.
But more than cash and a place to crash I was burned out,
bummed, drugged and half drunk, happy to land where
ambition could slumber even as my teenage coast-to-coast trip
continued haunting me. Nothing was the same
after that. Born in '52, I grew with the tube preaching
Mayberry and Real McCoys, always leaving
it to Beaver because Father Knows Best, never sure
what was real and what was not when Jack Ruby was shot,
Sullivan's Beatles loved me yeah, yeah, yeah
and Armstrong took his giant lunar leap.
But in '69 at seventeen I crossed
the summer-ripe country by thumb, television lies exploding
in my face. College that fall felt like cardboard
and I went through motions still possessed by the trip,
disenchanted with America's dream, finding authenticity in
the dump's random detritus
where affluence washed up like wave-tossed flotsam.

A meteor crashing into my world, it all came hurtling
back late one night when a clutch of teens
wandering and hungry for something happening
climbed the landfill fence with their own dreams
of a Prankster bus bought on EBay or Amazon,
places Abbie Hoffman never dreamed of stealing a book.

THUMBING

Thumbing across America's broad belly
was my *On the Road* Kerouac wet dream, riding the ribboned
pavement from little Westmoreland, CT to L.A.'s angelic
Hollywood fantasies. Crossing the Empire State line left
me weightless, wrested finally from home's
black-hole-gravity, soon over the Hudson with Half Moon
visions of Dutch sailors breathless at a new world's dense
greenery. Pennsylvania's thick woods and lumpy hollowed
out hills shadowed by coal piles
gave way to a world of small farms and church-spired
villages nestled in river valleys until I reached Ohio
which rolled like massive green sea swells quilted with trees
and dark, deep soil furrowed with corn
as far as Lake Michigan's shore
which pulsed with factories and belching smokestacks,
transmission lines, cloverleafs
and rail tracks as Chicago's shimmering cliffs came into view.
Rides took me through Lincoln's land playing Peoria
and crossing a muddy, roiling wide
Mississippi at St. Louis' shining steely horseshoe. Rocketing
though farm and field and crossroad towns to sprawling rail
yards at Kansas City, I was hypnotized
by spacious skies and wheat-edged cottonwood lined creeks
where blue heaven swallowed earth as the Rockies' pale,

jagged promise grew gradually larger until snow capped
peaks left Denver a model-train-table toy. Climbing
and winding, I cruised through thick aspen and pine along
jagged rock faces, the road a rollercoaster, rivers flowing
wildly far below and towns clinging to life in marginal places
near old mines whose tailing-scarred slopes bloomed
with color. South and west the rides barreled through dry,
wind sculpted canyons and vast red rock country, mesas
floating in endless azure as John Wayne roamed imagination
and multiple armed spiny saguaros horded water
until at last tangled roads and bronzed hillsides dotted
with homes flickered in the pallid gray light of Los Angeles.

In June I left my western Connecticut hill town
with maple-lined green, colonial houses and battered,
half empty riverside brick button factory beside a stone block
dam, launching into a world brimming with promise,
a *Whole Earth Catalog* of dreams. My parents
divorced three years, Dad on the left coast, Mom
couldn't stop me with demands, bus ticket pleading, and tears
after I told her my father thought thumbing
would make me a man. But planning to surprise,
wanting to take my time and exploding chances, I never spoke
to him, knocking on his door after ten days, a neighbor
saying he was away weeks building concrete foundation
forms on a big development somewhere near San Diego.

I imagined an Exodus from home leading to a promised land
of sweet liberty and pioneering adventure whose breath
of fresh air I'd tasted in '68 when I was clean
for Gene, passing out leaflets and making phone calls
from a faded Hartford storefront, urging
people to dump the Hump in the months
before our own Senator Ribicoff condemned Gestapo
tactics in Chicago streets. Despite defeat I was energized
by a man who stood up alone and made things happen,
rousing me to see the country he tried to save, fantasizing
events and people surging through me one ride
after another like a happy-ending *Easy Rider*.

I came back buzzing with stories, knapsack packed with hope.
Reborn, more real, my world pivoted on the cross-country
trip. America could be sculpted as easily as its clay soils,
could be hewn and shaped as skillfully
as its grand-tree logs. Change would blow like wind
on the plains, fulfilling Dylan's croaky-voiced promise
of *The Times*. I kept the faith
and signed petitions, preached my own *Strawberry Statement*,
went to teach-ins, led a first Earth Day hike,
hitched to Washington against the War in '71,
dipped into the Reflecting Pool, carried a placard
down Pennsylvania Avenue. In those years The Beatles
released their last, Laos was invaded, EPA warred on toxics
and waste, the Pentagon Papers hit the press,
Kubrick released his apocalyptic Clockwork
and voting began at eighteen. Ferment and foment,
America was greening in a Woodstock of liberated lifestyles,
meaningful music, primal pathways of thought, cheerfully
expressive clothing, consciousness expanding drugs,
and creative dissent leading to enduring wholeness.
A revolution of renewal free from the system's
grip was coming and I was there. We were ready to fly,
our hearts vibrating with a rush of self-righteous rage
and seeming magic in the daily routines of life,
believing ourselves at the very axis of experience.

Still wired into those years, music, ads, headlines
and catch phrases play a continuous brain loop,
an inescapable earworm rhythm reminding me the lost self
is still missing, the machine failed to self-destruct
and the corporate state rolled on feeding technology
fabricated lives. Are granola, tie dye tees, Birkenstocks,
homeschooling, long hair, rock and roll, and free range
organic foods our sole legacies? The only change I now
believe in are the nickels and dimes I get with grocery
receipts. Adventures seeming so meaningful and vibrant
are now so much wreckage washed up on the wrack line

of dreams, just more stuff bound for burial
at the dump where I secretly gloat over every load
of discarded junk on which a nation is choking.

Sure, I like meeting people and found an easy place to live
as one day faded into the next month quickly birthing years,
but maybe it was the trip, freighted with wrecked
hope that held me here at the raw, misspent end
of everything we make and believe. What will the future
say about we who imagined a future impossible to realize,
fed by an ethos teaching us to see in myth and Mandela
what is only sweat leading to flaccid skin and arthritic fingers.
We were fools and fooled, high on our own naïve hopes.
But could trip memories pave an open road
leading away from fear and loathing?
It would take those fence climbing kids
to get me thinking about thumbing again, riding pavement
out of the past, a time traveler
reaching back to find my way forward.

THE KIDS

Second of March, late night and cabin lights out,
a single bare bulb burning in the sugar shack.
I crouched by the arch and struck a match to kindling,
the stainless pan above filled with water-clear sap awaiting
the season's first boil. Flames filling the cast iron mouth
lit bright as a smile, I slammed heavy doors and watched
as pinprick bubbles grew to rumbling cauliflower
mounds churning to steam clouds rising to an open skylight.

Sitting back in a battered lawn chair salvaged from the fill,
I skimmed the newspaper, the small room filling with warmth
and sweet moisture, a serendipitous Yankee sauna.
Scooping foam from the raging pan, I heard voices outside
and grabbed a flashlight and brass poker.

At the fence fifty yards away I saw a shadow climb and jump,
landing with a thump beside others inside the eight-foot-high
barrier. Soft laughter echoed as they trotted
toward the mound while I quietly closed from behind.
Flicking the light, four mid teen boys darted like roaches
to the dark. "Justin Lamb, Ralph Ashton, Billy Chomski,
and Ronny Nosde," I shouted, shining
what must have felt like a stage beam on the teens.
"I know you and your parents too, so stop now

and there'll be no trouble. Over to the sugarhouse
on the double or a dry pan will start a fire
and more than your folks will come."

"We weren't doin' nothing, Mr. Dempster.
Just lookin' around," said freckled Justin Lamb
as I quickly opened the valves, pouring more sap
into an almost dry evaporator.

"Past midnight, you break in for nothing?"

"Just wanted to see if we could do it, and maybe check
out the big bear that's been chowing garbage.
Someone on Facebook said it's tipping six bills and has three
ear tags," replied Ralph, a heavy fifteen year-old with thick
glasses. "Plus they dared me and I even beat Billy."

"With a head start and better shoes!"
the athletic Chomski kid shot back.

"You're not going to squeal, are you.
We weren't out to hassle anything and with the house dark
and the dump open at seven on Saturday, we figured
you were sacked out" said squeaky voiced Ronny.

"Didn't count on sugaring season, boys,"
I half laughed. "I'm keeping some odd hours."

Silence settled as steam again began rising,
the boys a bit scared but also mesmerized by the curling gray
clouds hurrying for the skylight. Eyes traced the PVC feed
line of icy cold sap from a 250 gallon tank
up against the outside clapboards to where it met a copper
line wound around the boiler stack to warm
the liquid as it dripped into the pan. The fire's crack
and pop, the rumble of the boil and warm steam
induced a sweet hypnosis until at last cocky
Billy, a jock in three sports, broke the quiet.

"My Mom calls you a burnt out old hippie."

"So what if I am," I laughed.

"You've got the beard and pony tail.
Did you live in a commune
and go to protest marches, do LSD?"

"Do you listen to the Dead and the Doors?"
redheaded Justin asked. "We're kind of into them.
'Uncle John's Band,' 'Riders on the Storm,' you know.
And the Stones and Dylan.
I have my granddad's old albums. Their scratchy,
but I loaded the tunes on my I-Pod anyway."

"We heard you hitchhiked across the country," Ronny said.
"And so what if I did."

"Tell us about the sixties," Ralph said, placing hands on wide
hips. "Like you had the Beatles and Elvis,
Simon and Garfunkel, the Byrds."
"What about them," I said, waving a dismissive hand.
"Look at us with screamo, metalcore and emo. Who cares?
You had men landing on the moon and now space is just a
dune buggy on Mars. You saw 'Easy Rider'
and 'The Graduate,' but we got 'The Hangover' and 'Avatar.'
The country cared about Vietnam, but Iraq
and Afghanistan are like video games to lots of people."
"Yeah," Justin interrupted, "Obama's cardboard
compared to JFK, Bobby and Dr. King.
You had marches on Washington, sit-ins on campuses
like Columbia and happenings going down in Golden Gate
Park. Earth Day was a real deal. We can't even get kids
to sign a petition unless
it'll save them a few bucks or get 'em a free tat."

"What was it like?" Ronny chimed. "Living in this burb
sucks. It's dull as crap. Nothing real ever happens.
Being stuck here is a rip-off!"

Years of people trucking broken remnants
of their world to me,
I was flattered, forgetting when anyone had last asked
about my life. These boys were as eager as puppies,
hungry for something they thought only I had.
Knowing the forecast,
I sent them home with a promise to spin stories
of my cross-country trip if they'd be back at dusk in two
days to help collect sap and fire the evaporator.

AT THE EVAPORATOR WITH SENATOR MCCARTHY

Two nights in the twenties, sunny days reaching forty-five,
my buckets were brimming when the teens came noisy
and psyched. As if playing a game, they eagerly spilled
galvanized containers into plastic pails and then into a tank
in back of my truck, lifting and bending with rubbery ease.
Lining the dump road, the maples were a long gone
remnant of a dairy whose owner generations past
planted a colonnade and bought seed corn with proceeds
from a first crop of sugar. Pumping almost two hundred
gallons into the outside storage vat leaning against
the sugarhouse, we gathered in the cold shack as I lit the fire.

Flames leapt as I wondered if I'd promised just another dose
of poisonous hope. Who was I to play the cracker barrel
codger at the hearth, assuming a role as I might don a flannel
shirt and overalls? In the '60s we'd fooled ourselves
into thinking we were building a different world
to make a difference. Was I simply offering
bright-eyed kids infatuated with that past a glass of the same
intoxicating Kool-Aid of disappointment and disillusion?

But stories were promised, so we sat on upended chunks
of cordwood before the cast iron arch, open doors
favoring atmosphere over efficiency. Flames caught

as quickly as that sadly faded contagion of hope,
the firelight flickering on young faces seeming as malleable
as time makes stories. I felt glimmering warmth
on my cheeks, watching their skin grow ruddy
while fire roared and steam rose.

*Just old enough to drive in '68, I fretted over my draft number
and watched each night as Cronkite read the body count.
Two boys from town, KIA, already back in a box, shocking
a small place to have given so much.
One friend's brother, red hair and blue tinted
sunglasses, had taken off to Toronto and another worked
the system for C.O. status, finding himself a MEDIC in Nam,
twice wounded. Young men died while old men
made money and LBJ delivered speeches.*

*Lightning struck when a little known Minnesota senator
surprised pundits in New Hampshire's March primary.
By April, I was hitchhiking to Hartford on weekends
and then four times a week when classes ended.
High school and college kids vibrated with excitement
in a small storefront with windows papered in posters,
position statements and bumper stickers. Out from under
Mom's list of chores—garbage, the lawn and vacuuming—
and free from Mrs. Moore's algebra
and 200 words each week in Mr. Acker's English
class, I at last felt alive. Stay home, Mom pleaded
with worries about Hartford's dangers and temptations,
finally in frustration yelling
that "a vote for McCarthy was a vote for Ho Chi Minh."
But she only fueled desire, and each time I stuck out my thumb
was a declaration of independence.*

*I handed out leaflets and buttons, meeting and greeting
lunchtime office workers passing through or brown-bagging
in Bushnell Park, remembering always to smile, be polite
and accept refusals gladly. Evenings we'd stand
on the Isle-of-Safety where busses queued,*

*and hand our messages to the tired men and women
shuffling on board—cleaning ladies, bank tellers, waiters,
shop clerks and insurance company pencil pushers—weary
at day's end and usually glad for a smile.
Sometimes at factory gates in morning's thin light
we'd meet grim faced men grasping lunchboxes, few
of whom took our leaflets—Pratt or Colt,
a small machine shop or plating company.
I had a stake in the nation's fate, felt larger than I was, part
of something big, able to hold my own in street corner
conversations, knowing the war was wrong, that money
saved would rebuild America.
I was finally a person, not just someone's son.*

"Dude, you mean, like, you volunteered
for free?" Ralph asked.
"That's what volunteering means. Trust me,
believing in something mostly beats getting paid."

*Some days in the office we dialed with eight phones
at a table made from an old door stretched across saw horses.
We got lists of numbers from office manager Ed, a Trinity
College prof wearing half buttoned flowered shirts
who spoke with a fancy Boston accent.
He brought in a stereo, mostly to blast
his complete Dylan collection, including bootlegs like "Great
White Wonder" and "John Birch Society Blues."
A day didn't go by without both discs
of "Blonde on Blonde" at least three times. "Sad Eyed Lady
of the Lowlands" went on forever by the second spin
with Ed lecturing on traditions of poetic ballads dating
to Medieval times, causing snickers behind his back.*

*No voice mail or answering machines then, we'd call number
after number on rotaries, crossing off those we'd reached
and where they stood, if they'd say. Sometimes we got hang-
ups or cussed. I was called a Commie
and Viet Cong tool, but also found a couple new volunteers*

*and occasional encouraging words. Coffee perked
on a hot plate fueled our calls, and elderly Mrs. Pratt
delivered baked goods almost daily from her apartment a mile
away. She called us her "boys and girls" and trumpeted
news of her grandson living on a Manitoba commune
since his double digit draft number.
Full ash trays and a blue-gray haze filled the days.*

*Electric passion, a sense of mission and intriguing characters
left Westmoreland light years distant. Lasky, a bulky
ex-marine who'd been to Nam told of dank chaotic jungles
not knowing where shots were coming from, knife-sharp
pongee sticks, wading in rice paddies, cigar-like joints,
and dragging blood-spattered wounded to waiting choppers.
Ground you'd take one week, he said, was taken
back the next. No one knew where he lived,
and most mornings we found him sleeping on boxes in back.*

*"Shutterbug" cut his hair to work for Gene, earning his name
taking pictures with an ever-present Instamatic.
Allergic to fur, he was 4-F, the night before his physical
sleeping with a friend's five cats
and seeing the doctors when barely able to breathe. Bradley
was a black kid from East Hartford with the coolest afro,
and Audrey, a sophomore at UConn, was a math whiz
who memorized phone numbers. Thirty-something Peter talked
non-stop about cooking and the crepe pan he'd perfectly
seasoned, but never made us a meal,
consuming most of Mrs. Pratt's doughnuts and leaving
after a few weeks, caught smoking dope*

The last drops of sap dribbled into the evaporator.
Late into the night we'd boiled almost 200 gallons.
Maybe it was the routine of feeding the fire, hissing
and popping wood, or intoxicating sweet steam, but the boys
were entranced as my long forgotten memories arose
as if out of the mist. A time and place tossed away
with bellbottoms and vinyl 33s had returned

as surely as if I'd dug down into the landfill. Having listeners
seemed to bring the old events alive, zombies that might go
on forever without me. Though I'd lived
them, the stories had become no more real than fairy tales.
Haunted by my own past, I'd charged electrodes
of imagination wired to a Frankenstein.
But I was tired and out of sap. "Okay guys,
we're running dry. Let's call it a night."

"But, like dude, you told us nothing about hitching
cross-country," Justin said. "Yeah, you promised!"
Billy added, as if demanding a winning wager.
"That was going to be the best part," Ronny
said with a pleading hangdog look.

They weren't the cool kids, but good kids,
not looking for trouble but for something fateful
to happen, bound more by what they weren't
than what they were, sharing interest
in an era whose rushing torrent of change
almost seemed more real than the time in which they lived.
It drew me back as sure as the smell of mom's coffeecake
in the oven. Like them, I didn't hang with the gearheads,
greasers, jocks, brainiacs, or artsy types. Grasping
for an identity giving us street cred, we called ourselves freaks
and outsiders. Now shades of my younger
self had come calling. I couldn't turn them away.

"I'll spill my guts if you come back to collect sap
and chop wood," I offered, secretly eager to tell more.
"Be here after two cold nights and a warm, sunny day."

SUGAR ON SNOW

After a week, big snow and two warm days the boys
were back, the ground glowing beneath a gibbous moon.
Muscular Billy and dark haired Ralph split wood
beside the shack—oak, hickory and easily
cleaved hemlock. The others gathered sap
and collected a bucket of fresh snow.
All worked fast, and soon sat on their stumps like nested
fledglings eager for food. "Some of the gang from Hartford
headquarters had rides and others were hitching
to the convention," I began, bending with a match
to the kindling. "Gene wouldn't win, but we'd make noise
in Chicago streets and convince him to run on his own.
I was psyched to be part of it, but Mom refused to spring me,
so I watched the political circus on television, hatching
a plot to head cross country the next summer. Despite
my hopes and imaginings, when at last I left it wasn't all cool
dudes and crazy rides," I cautioned, attempting to damp
expectations, diminish imitations.
"Mostly it was as dull as boarding a Greyhound."

In the misting dawn, only a few cars took the I-84 ramp
at Danbury's downtown edge where most drivers were slicked
down guys in shirt and tie. Pacing and kicking impatiently
in roadside grass as cars passed, my boots darkened

*with dew. An hour slowly ticking and nothing happening
I risked cops, trying my luck up on the interstate
where whooshing traffic split the air at sixty-five.
When at last a station wagon stopped, the driver had to lay
on the horn, alarm clocking me out of a daydream.
Picking up my pack, I charged for the open passenger door.
"Christ! You want a ride or not," said a balding man
in a rumpled brown suit, lips dangling a cigarette.
"I'm heading across the Hudson, almost to Pennsylvania."*

*Tall, gaunt, bluish jowls, he drove a Ford Country Squire
filled with boxes, the cream colored dash shadowed
with nicotine above the ash tray. "People say it's risky
picking someone up what with all the violence
in the country," he said, "but I'm for giving young
folks a ride. Hell, you gotta get around somehow
when you're a kid short on cash. Besides, a salesman
needs conversation to keep him conscious."
He rolled down the window and curls of smoke flew
into the chatter as he flicked his butt and quickly
lit another with machine-like ease. "Smart not to start
with the cancer sticks, son," he said, after I refused.
"Dirty habit I picked up in the service, stationed
in Germany after the war with nothing
to do but pull drags and flirt with frauleins."*

"What's with all the shoeboxes in back?" I asked.

*"Samples to show stores," he said, running a hand
through strands of Brylcreemed hair. "Been in the business
twenty-one years, working for a company outta Mass.
Probably sold brands you've worn. Good quality,
but affordable stuff." I looked down at brightly polished
wingtips, the only part of his outfit that didn't look slept
in. "Real beauties aren't they. And hold a shine
like no tomorrow. Footwear may not seem like much,
but it's a livin' and I'm selling something everyone needs,"
he said with a smile and gently pointed finger.*

*"You probably think hawking shoes is bullshit, but they make
a difference in the way people see themselves and others.
You can tell lots about a person by their shoes."*

*"No matter." I shrugged. "It's cool,
but I'm not into judgmental and status seeking stuff."
We crossed the Appalachian Trail,
 passed signs for Stormville and Farmers Mills.*

*"You got me wrong. I'm not suggestin' people be phonies
and put on a pair just to impress, but shoes are a small
thing deserving attention. Not everyone drives a Caddy,
but even your average working stiff can afford good shoes.
You can be an individual, you know, and like you might say,
'do your own thing.'" I nodded as he fell silent,
his face worn and tired. A guy spending his time driving
around with order forms and shoes,
sacrificing his life to the system, just blew my mind.*

*"What turns you on about selling,"
I finally asked, fearing I'd hurt his feelings.*

*"Love the road," he began, a big Rotary Club grin
igniting his face, "seeing stuff dash past the window—
especially with the interstates and you don't have to slow
for every little shit town with gas pumps.
'Course, doesn't take the same skill as days racing over twisty
two lane blacktops and around trucks. I got time
to think my thoughts, no know-it-all boss
breathing down my back. Sure, there's lots of lonely nights
in cheap diners and fleabag motels, but it's a challenge.
May sound easy, but not everyone's got the goods.
And I'm selling something useful to businessmen, not tricking
housewives into buying brooms and brushes, you know."*

*I cracked the window, releasing smoke.
He'd probably seen too many westerns,
cowboy tall in the saddle, riding the range and rolling*

his own. Still, despite my stereotype, we had a scary
lot in common. Independent and into the road's freedom,
he grooved on its whatever-the-day-might-bring possibilities.
I'd never gotten into rapping with a guy
like this, and maybe you didn't have to rail against the system,
drop out and turn on, or be some kind hip of artist
to get something real from life.

Grabbing a stainless steel pail and turning a valve,
I drained syrup, steaming and golden. "Justin! Get that ladle
from the table," I said, pointing a finger, "and the spoons.
Ronny! Bring the bucket of snow." I drizzled hot syrup
over white crystals, watching them shrink
and turn taffy-like. The boys dug in, quickly
devouring the entire container while I drew off more syrup,
putting it aside to filter later.

"Was that shoe guy a bullshit artist or just real chill?"
Billy asked, licking the last sticky snow from his spoon.
"Just a plain Joe, neat because he turned
me on to the possibility that sharing rides with strangers
might get folks talking, lead to real change."
Justin stood up, stretched, and gestured with his thumb
like he was looking for a ride. "I think we should hit the road
and meet guys like that!" I shook my head. All I needed
was their parents tagging me with teaching their kids
to hitchhike. "Don't fool yourself. They weren't all so cool
or easy. I got picked up by nut cases firing guns
from windows, perverts, druggies and drunks
who thought they were piloting spaceships. I copped rides
in cars so rotten I could see macadam
moving beneath my feet at eighty miles an hour."

"So what was the weirdest ride?"
Ronny asked. I paused a moment, rambling
through memories, smiled and shook my head.
"Tell us," Justin demanded. "Too freaky,"
I said. "It was a pervert, wasn't it," Billy said. I just smiled.

"Go on and tell us. You think we don't know about this shit,
what with all the priests, toilet seat voyeurs, deviant
teachers and predatory internet porno dudes."
Ronny laughed. "We know more about this crap
than you do. Every school, scout troop, summer camp,
and sports team pours on the child protection and harassment
training until you want to puke. We'll keep
it on the d. l. and if anyone ever finds out we'll just say
you were warning us against hitchhiking." I took a deep
breath. "Come on and tell us already," Justin said.

*One long ride through Pennsylvania, then two quickies
and I was moving through Wheeling, hidden among deep
green hills with the gray-green river snaking
around them, homes and factories like storybook miniatures.
Almost dark, I flagged my first Ohio ride, a bright red Ford
Falcon that took me west to the land of fresh starts
where my mind ran old movie reels of settlers clearing
the wilderness and building log cabins. I asked the driver,
thirty-something with short dark hair
and a goatee, where he was going, but wind chatter
past the open window was all I heard.*

*I turned my head to hear, but he was silent, eyes tranced
on the road. One hand on the wheel, the other lay in his lap,
pants unzipped, stroking himself, slowly and steadily sliding
his cupped palm along the shaft. Should I look tough
or make like nothing was happening? I shifted
in my seat toward the door and wondered which backpack
pocket held my knife. Was he a tabloid madman
poised to attack, stab me and dump
the body like a garbage bag on some back road?
Why else had he picked me up? Thoughts ran over the speed
limit. Moving too fast to open the door and jump,
could I vault over the seat and grab
him from behind or wrestle away the wheel? Shirt stuck
to my body with cold sweat, muscles tensed
and my brain spinning, the driver hadn't changed rhythm,*

just stared straight at the road. One hand stayed steady
on the wheel, the other worked like a piston.
I prepared for a struggle to the death,
but he acted like I wasn't there. Greasy hair almost pasted
to his skull, he could have been a local mechanic,
short order cook or be stocking shelves at the A&P.

It seemed as if we'd crossed half the state before a big green
sign announced the next exit. "This is my stop," I said dry
throated, in as natural a tone as I could muster.
The Falcon slowed and pulled to the shoulder just before
the ramp. The driver didn't say a word, didn't turn to look
at me, didn't interrupt himself as I hurried
from the car and slammed the door.

Trembling on rubbery legs, I stood dazed
in tall grass a few moments, my stomach churning, stumbling
slightly as I stuck out my thumb,
not so much to cop a ride, but to do something.
Everyone does their own thing, I reassured myself,
and he didn't try to hurt me, but his single-minded
self-possession was unnerving. Did I really
want to meet all the people America had to offer?

I stood on the darkening interstate over half an hour
without luck. Drizzle began falling and cars seemed to sneer
with a hiss as they passed on the wet road. Light rain fell
and every hope for a ride was a spray of water leaving me wet
and cold. I jumped to stay warm, waved
my hands to be seen, but drivers were invisible in their pods
of darkness and vehicles seemed to move under their own
power. A lousy place, but I had to camp.

Sidling down a steep embankment, I slipped and fell back
on my hands, twisting a wrist on the slick grass.
Walking to a cornfield's edge, my feet
were sore and swollen in boots squeaking with water.
In a truck's fleeting headlights I saw corn stalks not yet knee

*high. With my flashlight, I found a spot to pitch my army
surplus pup tent. Aching for a fire,
there wasn't a dry twig so I comforted myself with fresh socks
and jeans and a wool shirt that had been my father's.
Though my head pounded from hunger, I was too tired
to cook, opening canned sardines, barely working the key
with stiff fingers. I gobbled down the far-away
caught fish as raindrops pelted the canvass and cars
whooshed past on the pavement above. Crawling
into my sleeping bag, I wondered what my mother
was watching on television. Though I'd decided
to leave home, I felt as abandoned as the shredded recaps
and rusty mufflers along the road's shoulder.
I was on my own.*

The boys were silent, staring at me glassy-eyed like children
at their first movie. Long minutes passed before a piece
of hemlock in the firebox popped like a shot and they jumped.
"That was creepy," Ronny said, the others nodding, itching
with discomfort. "What would you have done
if he hadn't let you out?" Ralph wanted to know.
"I would have grabbed the wheel and fought the weirdo,"
Billy said, flexing his arm. "Yeah, sure, mister
muscles," came a taunting chorus.

"What about the commune," Justin said. "You
told us you'd tell us about the commune." Turning a valve
on the evaporator, I shook my head. Did they want
these stories as lessons, entertainment,
or to see how they themselves fit in time's continuum?
My dull truth was fantastic to them, a big adventure.
And by their listening the stories
were breathing again for me, going from forgotten script
to stage play. What I'd kept to myself so long came alive
with an audience. As if emerging from some dark hollow,
I felt like I had a secret identity, an assumed name,
a throwback soul. "Sorry, we're out of sap and done for
tonight," I said. "And if I catch you guys scrolling

one of those stupefying smart phones just one more time,
we'll be done for good." Chunky Ralph quickly
stuffed his cell in a jacket pocket. Almost in unison
they nodded sheepishly,
said good night, and shut the door behind them.

GHOSTS AT NIGHT

Sleep was always tough during sugaring,
overtired and wired on adrenalin, but story
telling with the boys brought the past hurtling back,
crashing into me like a streaking comet. Snippets
of those years insinuated their way into me, running
like an old-time newsreel, a record playing over and over
again. I found fragments of advertising, political speeches,
taglines, songs, sayings, headlines and poems
circulating through me with my blood, as if each contraction
and relaxation of the heart gave rise to words
I couldn't possibly have remembered, but had lodged deeply.

VIETNAM HELD RESPONSIBLE FOR INFLATION

Take a puff... it's springtime

PEOPLE'S PARK: 270' X 450' OF CONFRONTATION

Increasing concern among some scientists that returning
astronauts may contaminate the earth with strange

NEGRO YOUTH KILLED IN HARRISBURG CLASH

Counting the cars on the New Jersey
Turnpike, they've all come

CHANGE FOR THE BETTER WITH ALCOA

All life is a drop of water

RATE OF PRICE RISE SLOWS

Oh his clothes were coarse and hopes were high
as he headed to the promised land

GI'S ARRIVING IN VIETNAM FIND WAR BEGINS
WITH PUNCHCARDS

Our career shop sees you in short, snappy summer moods

CHILE'S NATIONALIZATION PLAN HURTS ANACONDA STOCK

Stephanie Mills, 20, of Mills College in Oakland
concludes that the only "humane" thing she
could do was avoid having children

QUAKERS RENEW CAPITOL PROTEST

Now it all started two Thanksgivings ago

DORAL SAYS IT ALL IN TWO WORDS: TASTE ME

After 30 Volkswagens, Father Bittman Still Believes

VIOLENCE PANEL FEARS COLLEGES WILL BECOME
SCREENED AND GUARDED CAMPS

PARTLY CLOUDY

The season's end drawing near at April's approach,
we peered into buckets with flashlights, tossing cloudy sap
from warm microbial days and keeping the clear, finding
feather-winged moths or a few drowning ants from an ever
awakening world. Some buckets were piss yellow and others
greenish from trees breaking bud. Crazed, weather-driven
long nights and bull labor was ending with relief and sadness
as peeper frogs played their sleighbell background
soundtrack from thawed swamps.

Again, two boys back at the shack splitting wood
and laying the fire, the shards of chopping used for kindling
around a nest of newsprint. Only a hundred gallons
collected and slightly cloudy, we needed
to boil before morning or it would go bad with temps
into the 40s. A last boil before pulling taps
would make dark caramel syrup, exploding with flavor.

"This'll be our last night, boys," I said, striking a match
as their faces fell. They'd caught the sugarmaker's
high of frantic activity and careful
observation, though I was tired and as glad to see the season
go as I'd been to see it come five weeks ago.
"I wish we could do this year round,"

Ronny squeaked. "It's, like, we're really in the 60s, hanging
out in a hut and living off the land. Like, I'm grooving,"
he said with exaggerated drama that made them laugh.

"Soon we might be chilling in a bus and do the 60s whenever
we want," Justin said. "Yeah," Ralph added with a whistle.
"And we'll paint it all sorts of crazy colors, pull
out most of the seats, put in a stereo,
bean bag chairs, a fake Persian rug, and burn incense."
"We've been surfing the net for one," Justin said, answering
the question clouding my face. "Not one of the big ones,
just a short old school bus with automatic transmission."

"What about living off the land," Billy wanted to know,
"did you do it on your trip?" My smile widened, memories
flooding back. "After a fashion, I suppose.
I met up with .." Justin threw up his hands.
"You said you'd talk about the commune!"
Flames suddenly flared in the firebox and the cold evaporator
pan pinged with heat. "I'll get to the commune."

Somewhere in the midst of Kansas I got a ride in a '59 Chevy
with big fins, a junker listing to one side with shot shocks
and oil darkened exhaust. Behind the wheel was Sandoz
with wild tangled blond dandelion-like hair, a madman's grin
and the infectious laugh of a demented myna bird.

The ground's slight roll became table flat under a vast sky,
the view limited by eyesight and imagination where fortress-
like gray concrete grain elevators seemed visible forever.
Trees clustered only around homes and along river banks
and orchards of oil wells sprouted instead. Openness
made us crazy and we joyfully yelled
at each other like shout-outs in a an old timey church.
Ticking off town names on the straight and flat we screamed
them back and forth like balls in a game of catch:
Homer, Dorrance, Ogallah, Grainfield, Mingo

*we called on the way to Kanorado. We whooped
and bellowed ideas and visions, snapshots of the mind,
a camera working in our heads.*

*"Take me to Kansas, to flatlands where grasses wave
like grandmas at train stations," I screamed red faced.
"The land rambles like gossiping women, and sun
fries the mind," Sandoz returned at the top of his lungs.
"Give me gravel roads at pure right angles."
"And tumbleweed beards clinging to highway fences."
Laughter was punctuation
as we grew hoarse roaring over window chatter.
"Let oil wells pump, let them fuck mother earth."
"Maps lie, earth expands, boundaries become lost."
"Natty Bumpo, American, lies buried here,"
I shouted in the pompous affectation of my history teacher.
"Ah, welcome to 'Midway America,'"
Sandoz said softly, finally out of breath. My throat ached, lips
chapped. Sandoz lapsed into white-line-fever.*

*Sudden brakes, a jerk, and fishtailing like we'd blown a tire.
Thrown to the dash and against the door
I looked out on empty grain fields.
"Gonna pick up some dinner," Sandoz grinned with a maniacal laugh.
"We're going hunting!" He headed down the pavement
behind the car, walking with exaggerated stealth as if stalking
game. Abruptly stopping, he raised his arm rifle-like,
making guttural sounds as if shooting the dead pheasant
lying at roadside, its feathers sparkling iridescently in intense
sun, its long tail graceful even in death.
"Neck's broken," said Sandoz matter-of-factly. "Poor birds
get hit all the time. Dead not more than an hour, I'd guess.
Pheasant on the menu tonight!" he cheered.
I shrugged. "You sure it's good to eat?"
I asked. Sandoz unleashed a big laugh.
"Better put on your best duds for some fancy grub."
Twenty miles later, two more birds in the trunk.*

WELCOME TO COLORADO, a gigantic road sign
proclaimed in bright metallic blue and yellow.
Expecting sudden snow capped peaks, the land
only grew flatter and drier. Kansas, only more so.
With eye-squinting headaches, we did like movie cowboys,
heading west into a red fireball of sun for what seemed hours.

I pointed out huge clouds on the horizon, but Sandoz shouted:
"No! No! No! Mountains! Mountains! Mountains!"
We tossed the word back and forth like a mantra, every breath
bringing renewed energy as shadows grew to massive
pieces of hard rock—profiles of power, distinct ridges
and peaks, summits shoulder to shoulder.
"America's massive tits rising from her flat,
sexy belly," Sandoz screamed. Sun dropping behind
them, the sky glowed like a church window:
orange and purple with hovering clouds
in lacy red strips. The land began slightly rolling.

Darkness settling, we barreled down the interstate
through Denver where downtown towers were lit rectangular
lamps and street and houselights twinkled like a linear
galaxy along the base of the Rockies.
Straight for the mountains at 75, the road
launched us through a cleft of shadowed rock and soon city
lights yielded to hot stars as Sandoz drove
mechanically on, his features smoothed in the night,
road dirt and sweat bathed away. Ears clogged and popped.
The car whined, straining on the long, steep incline.
In artificial daylight with hollow echoes we torpedoed
through a tunnel, and back in darkness
I turned to see the lit tube like a silhouette inside out.
Now we were beyond whatever was behind us, in new country
floating visions of miners, loggers, prospectors
and trappers. We were finally west, on the other side.

Sandoz began nodding, and at Silverthorne
we took Route 9 north about ten winding miles as my lids,

*too, turned leaden. At a sharp turn on a dirt track
that opened out of nowhere,
I asked where we were. "Shit if I know,"
Sandoz said. "These hills are snaked with old logging
and mining roads. I'm on fucking radar, man. Need to catch
some zees." Climbing gradually on a jaw rattling ride
over rocks and rain-dug gullies, branches
scraped the car flinging twigs and needles as we rode
wheel ruts until hitting a grassy
clearing where a sudden stop left astounding quiet.*

*"I'll get to cleaning these birds,"
Sandoz said, opening the door to chill air.
"You check out some wood and find a few fire ring rocks.
Aspen burns better than pine." Wandering in starlit dark,
I found a charred bare spot and gathered
a couple armfuls of wood while stumbling along the treeline.
Brittle kindling sticks teepee style over a nest
of dryer lint kept in my pack, I struck
a white capped kitchen match on my zipper. Flames leapt
as I cracked larger sticks across my knee. With crisp
snapping wood and honest smoke
we were getting down to basics,
finding our way to a better world where things were real.*

*Staring into flames, I saw Sandoz outlined in wavering light,
brightening and dimming with the breeze. Perched on a rock,
his gaunt face sunburned by firelight,
he easily pulled pheasant feathers, and bits of down floated
away like milkweed fluff. Borrowing my knife,
he severed the head and slit the belly, grabbing the squishy
entrails and tossing them onto the fire to sizzle and pop,
my mouth watering with barbecued chicken memories
as I wondered where he learned all that Boy Scout stuff.
Coals glowing, Sandoz cut several "Y" crotched live
branches, setting the birds on spits. From the car
he got a military mess kit and a dark green wine*

bottle. We sat on a log and I attacked the vino with my pocket
knife corkscrew as he rolled a couple joints.

"That's living off the land while on the thumb,"
I said, adjusting the sap flow.
"Sweet," Ronny whistled though his teeth.
"You can put me down for some of that!"
Billy asked how pheasant tasted. "Same as chicken,"
I said, flapping my arms to big laughs. "Like, did you ever
do living off the land again, I mean on the trip?"
Ralph wanted to know. "Dumpster dived for breakfast
with some street people in Denver," I told him. "And Sandoz
would go into diners just after rush hour, sit at an uncleared
table and chow leftovers." Ralph made a face.
"Yuck! That's gross."
Ronny put a gagging finger to his mouth.

*Just after lunch, we walked into a Phoenix storefront,
its large sign with sword-crossed fork and spoon, crimson
"EAT" in bold letters. Lots of small tables, many with dirty
dishes on white-and-red-check tablecloths,
and a few lingering customers sipping from steaming mugs.
Sandoz moved quickly, sitting at a plate of limp salad,
a partially eaten roll and slightly congealed stew
which he devoured like a starved animal.*
"Aren't you hungry?" he asked.
"Famished, but not for this shit,"
I said, looking at a cold half Rueben with crescent bites.
"Last stand of a gourmet or you just came into big money?"
He grabbed the sandwich.
"The person before us could be sick,"
I said. Sandoz shook his head.
"Okay Mr. Health Inspector. Just not hungry enough, huh, "
he replied, mouth full. "Man, you gotta loosen up,
chuck the excuses. Life isn't some uptight beat philosophy
from some book or flick. We gotta be tough to crash
the machine." *He hopped to the next table,
wolfing down a soggy slice of toast and few home fries*

*beside a coagulated pool of egg yolk. A ponytailed high
school girl approached with menus. "Just a coffee,"
Sandoz said to her with a Cheshire cat grin.
Hungry, I ordered a tuna fish sandwich
with fries, leaving a big dent in what little cash I'd stashed.*

"I finally got into leftover hopping after the third time,
and it wasn't so bad 'cause I was starving and broke
as I sat down to the lion's share of a super-sized steak.
Didn't get it all, though. A counterman with big biceps
and blue tattoos got pissed because he took scraps
for his dogs." I slapped a hand on the hollow
sounding sap tank. "That's all for today, boys.
So little left, I'll finish it on the kitchen stove."

"Rip off!" Justin shouted. "Nothing on the commune?"
"Come back next week and help clean up," I Tom Sawyered.

MORE GHOSTS

Not long after the boys left, ghosts settled around me again,
seducing me like the smell of baking bread
or fresh brewed coffee. Helplessly enveloped,
I succumbed to their hypnotic phrases
and long gone but irresistible rhythms
that felt almost like sleep.

ANTI-WAR SAILOR TRAILED BY 25 AGENTS

He can't do it, he can't change things
It's been going on for ten thousand

CLEAVER CHEERED IN ALGIERS

A revolutionary new process lets him shampoo
a full head of hair without transplants

BIG BOARD PRICES DECLINE SHARPLY

Why wait any longer for the world to begin
You can have your cake and

DOING THE WASH

Warm and sunny, buds fat on branches and some small
Leaves unfolding like tiny hands, the boys set rows of buckets
outside the sugarhouse, dipping each in a barrel of sanitizing
solution and scrubbing with a bristling round brush before
bathing three times in water. Lifting the evaporator pan
off the arch, we scoured its long, narrow channels
and scraped the black burnt carbon build-up from the bottom,
coal-like dust painting everything it touched. The firebox
was swept of ash, the sticky sugarhouse floor mopped.

Sun halfway swallowed at the horizon, sinking blood
red beneath an orange sky, Sandoz and I pulled into a rutted
driveway at a rolling, almost treeless place with rough
grasses and shrubs in faded greens and browns
where domes of triangular sheet metal squatted like starships
from another planet. Bright greens, pinks, reds, blues,
and purples caught the last light, and periscope-like
stovepipes rose from these igloo prisms.
"This is a Self- Proclaimed Butterfly Sanctuary,"
a sign warned near a yellow mailbox.
"Where are we?" I asked Sandoz.
"Drop City, man. Like tune in, turn on, drop out—you dig?"

Grocery sacks in hand, stuff Sandoz "liberated"
from a Safeway like a shadow Abbie Hoffman or Jerry Rubin,

*we headed to the big kitchen dome figuring folks
were gathered for dinner. A bag beneath each arm,
we felt like suburbanites returning home
from the supermarket. "They got some kind of design award
and each dome shape has a special name,"
Sandoz was saying, "like that kind of stretched out one—
that's a zome, used as the outhouse. Just pieces cut from junk
cars nailed to wood frames—that's why all the far-out colors.
It's like they laid waste to the American dream
machine, gave the finger to the system. The kitchen dome
is something Peter Rabbit calls a rhomboicosocodecahedron.
He's the resident sage and caretaker, the soul of Drop
just because he's been here long enough to see some changes
go down." The place radiated like a smile.
I'd found the future.*

*Entering the big dome burrowed into a hillside,
we walked through a shop cluttered with tools
and a room with a long shelf of books and records
while singing wafted up from below. Down a staircase
we entered a kitchen where twenty people clustered around
a long pine table. A frontiersman-looking guy with a wild
auburn beard and red plaid flannel shirt sat on a crate
strumming guitar while others played harmonica, mouth harp
or banged on pots. A big breasted woman added fiddle
notes as the rest sang and clapped. Setting the bags
on a small side table, Sandoz chuckled and turned
to me: "You won't believe this, man, but I recognize only
one guy from last year and don't even know him.
Thought to see at least Luke Cool, Suzie or Curly.
Oh well, welcome to Butterflyville."
He walked over to the table and joined the singing:
"This land is your land, this land is my land,
from the redwood forest to . . ."*

*No one appeared to sense anything unusual and a round
faced girl with sparkling hazel eyes and braided hair
walked by, said hello and hugged me like an old friend.*

*She emptied the groceries into dented white enamel cabinets
and a rusting cooler as if expecting a delivery.
I sat beside Sandoz on a bright blue plastic milk crate
and joined the singing. We faced a beautifully stitched
tapestry stretching across the wall with black, brown
and green Native American geometrics. Unfamiliar lyrics
about a no trespassing sign and hungry people were sung
to Woody's familiar tune, and my life seemed rainwashed.*

"Ronny and Ralph, let's lift the pan back onto the arch,"
I said, pointing at the stainless rectangle. "It's heavy, but try
putting it down easy. Run some sanitizer through these feed
lines, will you, Billy, and then flush them with water,"
I said, tapping the white PVC pipe with my foot.
"So you really were at a commune,"
Ronny said with high pitched amazement
suitable to news of a moon voyage.
Suddenly the opening notes of "Sympathy for the Devil,"
with its hypnotic percussive rhythm, exploded
in the sugarhouse. "Shit!" Ronny said, his face
reddening as he reached into his pocket to squelch
his cell. "Sorry," was all he could say to our laughter.

I could fool them with made-up stuff
up and they'd never know, but I didn't need
to. They thought they lived in a lusterless age,
and dreamed of bygone decades. Still, all it amounted
to was a bunch of stories, things so far from what really
mattered they might as well be fiction; events,
ideas and visions that, as it turned out, were as ineffectual
as the boys imagined their own lives. They failed
to see me frozen in time, how the hope of those years
left a residue of paralysis. How could I tell them about
the expanse between who I was now and who I wanted be?
It was as real as the space between atoms and about as easy
to see. Was I a Rip Van Winkle snoozing away
my years sleepwalking at the dump? What else
could I do now but tell stories even as I felt suckered

by them? I was speaking in tongues,
channeling my past, charming myself with the sound
of my own voice. Maybe it wasn't so much the tales
as the telling. If these kids
were glued to the words perhaps they really meant something,
or was it just so much emotional euthanasia?

*I awoke to a scratchy Donovan record, its high fluted
notes floating from a speaker in another room. Columns
of sunlight spilled into the loft where Sandoz
and I were crashed on lumpy, sheetless mattresses.
We'd racked late after "Mom's Disposable Backyard Band"
played itself out for the night. I was wrecked
from hours of singing, clapping, laughing, and passing an old
water-filled whisky bottle that made the evening more magical
than booze could. Joints continuously circled the room,
and every breath seemed to wobble the planet
taking me higher in the smoke filled space. Sandoz
was still breathing rhythmically, his face sweetly
nestled in the crook of his arm.*

*Sun stinging light ricocheted off the car panels and lit copses
of brushy trees and khaki grasses as I walked to the outhouse
through a world of stark light and shadow, like a photo
on high contrast paper. An air force of flies
took off and buzzed as I approached, nervously
landing and alighting again. Opening the door, waves
of stale urine stench hit me like a sucker punch and I gagged,
holding my breath as the hot yellow stream flowed. The pit
overflowed with hideous lumps and logs, the floor piss
soaked. Why, I wondered, didn't anyone do something?*

*A big burly guy with a bushy beard and dark, stringy hair
in a ponytail was flipping pancakes in the kitchen.
With heavy cycle boots and a belt-loop-chained wallet,
Woodchuck seemed a Hell's Angel gone hip
as he worked like a seasoned chef. Almost 9:30, I hadn't seen
anyone else. The Donovan record clicked off and the changer*

*dropped an Allman Brothers album. I asked if the rest
of the folks were working the fields. He looked puzzled,
so I asked if the others were watering crops before the sun
got too high. "You mean the garden?"
he asked, scratching his beard. "Eat and I'll show you."*

Woodchuck finished, wiped a big sheath knife on his pants,
holstered it on his belt and tossed his fork onto the plate,
adding to a teetering pile in the sink. "So, you want to check
out the garden," he said, as if doing me a favor.
Bringing over my own plate, I started cleaning some dishes,
thinking it payment for a night's sleep and some grub.
"Whatever you're into, man," Woodchuck said with a shrug,
"but don't hassle it. They always get done somehow."
He left to put a Stones album on the stereo
and when he returned I asked for soap. He looked
as if I'd lapsed into a foreign language. "Nah, no soap.
Stuff got used up weeks ago." Washing with just water,
I only spread the grease. "You ready, man,"
Woodchuck wanted to know.

Ten feet by ten, the garden was fenced with string strung
between tomato stakes. The ground had been turned over,
but was dry and cracked, arid rows and a cluster
of dusty mounds the only evidence that someone
had thought of gardening where pigweed and dry grass
were growing poorly. "Some guy blew
through here a while ago and started this thing,"
Woodchuck explained, "but I don't know
much about it because I wasn't here then."

* * *

Sitting in the shade of a large dome, I sucked on grass
stalks and watched Drop City come alive. Everyone seemed
to wear some army surplus stuff—green cargo pants, Ike
jackets, khaki shirts with chevrons—along with tie-dye
and jeans. Three guys started pounding nails

into what Woodchuck said was a chicken coop,
a couple left and someone else picked up one of the hammers.
The first Dropper took off and a few minutes later four new
guys were at it, one with a saw.
Like a jigsaw puzzle left on the coffee table of a large
household, the framing went up as hours passed.

Awakened late in the day, still with grass between my teeth,
I looked up at a tall, thin blond guy with a face so delicate
and cheek bones so high that but for his voice
I would have thought him a chick. "I'm Frodo. Woodchuck
said you were bummed by the garden. Let me show
you what Drop is all about," he smiled. Following him past
the kitchen, we came to a spacious one room dome
furnished only with a bunk and oak chest, but cluttered
with paintings on canvass, metal scraps, cardboard,
woodblocks and shells in bright splashes of color
swirling with movement. An easel stood in a pool of sun
pouring from a skylight, paints and brushes scattered.
"This is what Drop City is all about. Instead of farming
we do droppings, bringing art to life and life to art
until there's no distinction between the two.
We build awareness by taking junk and trash
and getting people to see in a new way.
Garbage is a resource
and we've created an America free zone,"
he said, folding arms across his chest, "a launch pad,
testing ground, full time life-sized experiment."

*   *   *

Nothing since breakfast and starving by five,
I headed to the kitchen dome and found one of the apples
we'd brought. Van Ronk was accentuating the positive
on the stereo. With two big windows, the kitchen filled
with light making flowers painted on the wall
as vivid as a garden. The floor was dirty, the stove shiny
with grease, and I had been last to wash a dish. Drop

worked in a neat way, but if everyone pitched in with chores,
living could be so much easier. Would that disrupt the vibe?
Don't act like some big time parent
and impose your own trip, I scolded myself. Go with the flow.

Down to core and stem, I laid the apple on the table
as a skinny dude, long straight brown hair parted
on the side, walked in with a couple soiled grocery bags.
Barefoot and wearing only faded Levis unraveled
in both seat and knees, his chest was a ladder of ribs.
"Great hunting party, man! Got real goodies from the old
Safeway today!" he announced, pulling out several heads
of limp lettuce, some carrots, potatoes and other dumpster
gleaned produce. He handed me a couple loaves
of bread with a few tiny gray-green dots of mold,
as if I knew where they'd go. I turned and he was gone.

The apple core slowly browned. A blond woman
in a long paisley skirt, orange tee shirt and pig tails
bounded into the room. She asked if I'd start chopping
vegetables as she rummaged around for some rice.
With rot spots cut away the produce didn't look so bad.
I was peeling carrots when Frodo came by with Northstar,
a woman whose jeans were entirely bright patches.
She grabbed ingredients from the cabinets and began
kneading bread with long, slender fingers. Frodo passed
a joint as he poked in the fridge. "We're doing some grain
and veggie thing tonight," the woman in the paisley skirt
announced, exhaling a deep toke. "Only a little rice, but
we've got pasta, too."

With dinner almost done, the room filled with laughter
and chat. No appointed hour to eat, but somehow everyone
knew. On the table I put a big wooden bowl filled with grain
and glossy veggies stir fried in soy. Sitting on a long bench,
I suddenly realized that I alone worked at making dinner
from start to finish. Perched next to Sandoz
as the water-filled whisky bottle went around for all to swig,

*I saw the usual nervous energy rocking his body,
inhabiting the space around him. That eternal grin lit his face
as he played with a coin, bouncing and flipping it, making
it disappear up his sleeve or behind his ear—anything to stay
in motion. No heavy raps commandeered the meal
and conversation was a savory spice with no parental bullshit
about talking with a mouthful or elbows on the table.
For the first time, I found joy not just in food,
but in eating. Dogs cruised for handouts,
occasionally barking, and no one seemed to notice.*

*"So freaky about how things get done around here. Stuff
just happens," I said to Sandoz. He nodded. "Feel
the energy," he said. "This is why corporate America
is coming down. No games. Everything's up front.
You know what's going down and if someone is trapped
in some pseudo game everyone can dig it because it's out
in the open." Taking a couple forkfuls,
I turned back to him. "It's so cool
that you don't have to be scared of being yourself.
It'd be perfect if they could just keep the outhouse
clean and were better organized in the kitchen and . . . ."*

*"Man, how many times do I have to lay
it on you to take a break from that middle class crap,"
Sandoz said sternly. "You think you're hip, but your cage
gets rattled whenever something scrapes against
your suburban scene." My eyes darted around the room.
Sandoz was his usual loud self and it seemed everyone
had heard and was staring. The space got close. Fogged
on grass, faces became funhouse distortions. "Lighten
up a little," Sandoz suggested. "That attitude
messes with your head." I nodded, shoveling a few forkfuls
into my mouth. I had long hair, wore bellbottoms,
smoked dope, was into the Stones and Dead, and served hours
of high school detention for protesting the war.
What was wrong with a clean place to shit?
Why couldn't I be as natural as Sandoz? Stuff going down*

at Drop was beautiful, but I was hassled.
If I couldn't make it here, would things ever happen for me?

"Was that the end? Did you leave?" Ronny wanted to know.
"I stayed for another week, until one morning
without warning when everyone was sleeping Sandoz
got the jitters and we lit out. "Dude, like you were an outsider
among the outsiders," Justin said. I shrugged.

"Before we made love one night, Northstar
told me that Drop wasn't as far out as straight people
or even the freaks thought because the country was settled
and built by outsiders, folks who got squirrelly
hanging too long in one place. Discovering Drop
was a process where people came and went,
got into it and didn't worry so much about things that bug
you when you're committed without end. I banged nails
into the chicken coop, helped Woodchuck with some machine
part sculptures, and climbed a nearby hill with a dozen
others on a birthday party picnic for a guy named Cody.
When we got to the top, no one knew
where Cody was, but it wasn't his birthday anyway."

When we'd laid out the picnic on a brightly striped Mexican
blanket, I turned to find the others tossing their clothes
and not knowing what to do, I did the same. Nakedness
was delicious in the day's warmth. It made time palpable
in a powerful conversation of bare skin.
I felt part of something, pretensions and fears melting
into the rumpled pile of clothing. The meal was mellow,
a family gathering lacking heavy raps or hip philosophy.
We talked about weather, the half built chicken coop,
a recent dumpster raid on Trinidad's Safeway.
Cheese bit my tongue, curry spiced my lips, cauliflower
was cool, and wine sweet. My eyes fed on rock textures, grass
and bodies. My ears savored birds and breezes
and I breathed the pines. It was so real.

GHOSTS AGAIN

They came back again like the echo
   of a loud sound or the aftertaste of something eaten hours
   earlier. The telltale phrases that wouldn't die,
the zombie undead words from the past returning
to haunt, keep me awake like a grandly snoring lover.
Again words sang as they circulated
in my veins, throbbed in my ears like breath after a hard run.

NIXON'S DECISION TO WITHDRAW
TROOPS SEEN IRREVERSIBLE

Virgin Islands rum—the next best thing to being there

NATIONAL DRIVE TO BAN DDT OPENS

Ramrod stiff, but with the old warrior's slow, healthy gait,
Omar Bradley, 76, walked across the Normandy field gazing
somberly upon the long orderly row of white crosses

THOUSANDS LINE UP TO VIEW
JUDY GARLAND'S BODY

Without a portable on vacation how will you know
what you're getting away from

ALCU TESTS WIRETAPS BY FBI OF GROUPS IN U.S

Tricia Nixon was, clearly, as London's admiring Daily Sketch put it, "America's Little Princess"

ARE MILLIONS CHANGING TO ELECTRIC
HEAT JUST TO SAVE MONEY

She does not bother, she knows too much to argue or to

YOU CAN TAKE THE PULSE OF PROGRESS
AT REPUPLIC STEEL

Dropping a stick before the couple, the pastor pronounced the legal essentials in mod vernacular: "You're married as long as you dig it"

POLL IN SOVIET FINDS DESIRE
FOR AUTOS IS A FETISH

Jackie spent more on family expenses, including $40,000 for clothes, in 1961, than Jack made as president

TELL SOMEONE ABOUT LARK"S GAS-TRAP FILTER

THIRD BASE

On my usual stool, I sat with elbows leaning into the shiny
black marble counter where I perched three times
a week, once for breakfast twice for dinner at the Third Base
Diner whose pretzeled neon sign above a streamlined
stainless skin proclaimed: "For a Meal Closest to Home."
I chatted about the Red Sox poor prospects with owner Nicky
Kakridis as he worked the grill with a ballet dancer's grace
and platoon commander's authority. The griddle sizzled
around the spatchula's percussive scrape as he turned eggs,
tended grilled cheese, fried bacon and sausage links.
He'd shuffle the batting order, send manager Valentine
packing and rest ~~righty~~ *lefty* slugger Ortiz with his bum wheels.

Fifteen stools, still half full late on a Tuesday morning,
the place hummed with conversation about upcoming
elections and a school's construction. At the counter's end
with a coffee was Nicky's dad, old Ari, who had the place
shipped from Jersey in 1950 to its spot on the green
between a brownstone and brick town hall and white
clapboard library with tall columns, a site where a colonial
house become an office had burned years earlier.
A little worn with time, it was still a gleaming eatery with sky
blue terrazzo floors, cobalt upholstery, and gray
panels on a barrel ceiling.

Only five-foot-four, dried and sunken in his 80s, Ari
had been a dynamo back in the day, wiry and strong, living
in a Macedonian cave two years fighting the Nazis
before stowing on a New York bound freighter,
working like a demon and saving for this dream. Legendary
for besting two gun toting robbers back in '71, he made
like he was going for the register, instead pulling a heavy
glass sugar canister from beneath the counter
and hitting the gunman on the temple sending him running,
his revolver flying. Quickly grabbing the second guy
twice his size, he beat the crap out of him
as the dishwasher dialed the cops. Hammering the man
within an inch of life, Ari was arrested but charges
were dropped. Now, with eyesight fading
and Nicky's mom gone a decade, he sat on his stool
like an oracle, still quick with a story or quip, telling a boy
last year that he'd double date him at the prom
if the kid would go to the cemetery and shovel
out one of Ari's old girlfriends. Would I wind up like the old
man, sitting on a salvaged lawn chair
in front of the dump's office trailer telling stories?

Breakfast was always black coffee, two eggs over easy
on a pancake, home fries and a double helping of the corned
beef hash Nicky ground from boiled Irish dinners
left after Monday's special. "Pitching is key,"
I was telling him, "fresh arms—a good setup man
and a closer, at least two decent starters, a righty
and a southpaw." Nicky turned from the grill
where he was laying out lettuce
and tomato for three BLTs and flashed
me a skeptical look as he spread mayo on toast.
Before he could answer,
Mickey Lamb was coming at me from a booth at the far end,
having just peeled off some bills for his check.

"Leave my kid alone," he said, sticking a big
finger in my chest.

"Back off," I said, brushing the finger away.

"You back off and keep away from my kid."
His voice grew louder with each word, his breath
full of Nicky's onion omelet.
"Stop filling his head with your tie-dyed hippie crap.
You work in garbage and serve it to him and his friends dirtier
than you got it." Lamb was a big guy with bulldog cheeks
and dark hair. A local contractor, he was built like a boxer,
raced at Lime Rock and had a sixth sense about machines.
"I don't want him coming home and telling me about your trip
to Woodstock, banging a bunch of braless
broads and smoking pot."

"What are you talking about? I never was at Woodstock.
And everything I've told them is true." His eyes
focused with anger, a vein pulsed on his forehead.

"I don't care if it's true or not, it's still bullshit,"
he shouted. "When Justin goes on eBay and buys a short
school bus he wants to paint psychedelic colors
and drive around like a yahoo, I know where the inspiration
comes from." I put my hands into a timeout T.

"First of all, I can't stop Justin and his buddies
from coming to the dump. It's public property. Second,
those kids were into the whole sixties
scene long before talking to me—music, clothes, lingo,
the works—and you know it. And it's a lot better
than some of the shit high schoolers get into today.
He's your kid. If you don't want him there, just tell
him to stay away." Lamb stuck his finger in my chest again.
"Oh yeah, that's your wet dream. You know full well
that dad coming down heavy will just
make him want it more. I'm warning you, this is going . . . ."

A palm pressed against my shoulder.
Nicky pushed us apart.
"You stay out of this. It's not about you," Lamb said.

"Had your meal, glad you enjoyed it. Now's time to go.
Let Caleb finish breakfast in peace." Lamb reared
up like a bear, thumbs in belt loops.
"I told you this is between me and Dempster.
It's got nothing to do with you."
Nicky glanced down the counter.
"You're upsetting my father, so please go."
Lamb took a deep breath. "Okay, but just for your father.
As for you," he said turning toward me, "better lay off
my kid, 'cause I'm not done."

TOMATOES, PEPPERS AND EGGPLANT

Sunday checking cold frames and a mini greenhouse
    built with windows and boards salvaged from the bulky waste
    pile, I was a general reviewing troops, tiny green plants
poking through soil sheltered under moisture beaded glass
these long weeks since sugaring season ended.
In rows and clusters were cucumbers (Orient Express, Straight
8, Spacemaster), eggplants (Black Beauty, Pingtung Long),
peppers (California Wonder, Diamond Bell, Sunrise Orange)
and my beloved heirloom tomatoes (Early Bush Beefsteak,
Prairie Fire, Prudens Purple, Brandywine Red,
Black Krim, Bellstar). I fought the itch to plant,
the back of my neck burning with the sun's fresh warmth,
cloying humidity filling every breath with rotting soil smell.
But not quite mid-May, a frosty night or two still
lurked like a thief before Memorial Day.

Retrieving my pitchfork from the shed, I sliced the tines
into soft ground, a sacrament suffusing with me with hope,
earth connection, strength in simple work
joining me to generations. Strain in my back,
perspiration leaking down my arms brought gardening
to godliness, a creation adjacent to Eden. Already seeds
were feeding me with Sugar Snap and Snow Wind Peas
climbing trellises of tossed off pallets, orderly
rows thick with German Giant

and Cherry Bell radishes, rosettes of Buttercrunch
and Blushed Butter Oak lettuce.

Running a hand across a sweat-beaded forehead
and looking up as I leaned on the fork, I saw Justin cycling
down the maple lined gravel road with Ralph struggling
behind him, a dinner-plate-wide smile, wildly
waving his hands like semaphore flags.
They'd been MIA since the evaporator was put to bed,
the buckets dried and stacked. My belly tensed
remembering his father's threats and fist tightened face
at Third Base. But they were through the gate
and beside me before I sorted delight of a drop-in visit
from anger and guilt at Mickey's intimidation.

"Hey, Mr. Dempster!" Justin shouted, walking up quickly
and out of breath, dropping the battered Columbia ten-speed
I'd plucked months ago from the metal bin. "Wanted
you to know we're following in your footsteps."
I swallowed hard, my throat suddenly dry and tight.
Had he bought the psychedelic bus?
What sex-drugs-and-rock-and-roll adventure was afoot
that would cause Mickey to blow like Fourth of July
and trace the lit fuse to me? Winded Ralph arrived moments
later, straight dark hair grown to brush his shoulders,
thick tortoise shell glasses traded for copper wire aviators.

"Back to two wheels? Thought you guys would never
give up the gas pedal once you got the feel." Ralph rolled
his eyes. "Lamby's idea," he said, catching his breath
and pointing a finger. "My mom's got the car and we
could've had his pop's pickup but . . . ." Justin clapped his hands.
"We're on a campaign to save the earth
and we have to do more than talk the talk!
That's what we want to tell you about."

"We're going join a political campaign,
just like you did for McCarthy. We'll change things

for the better, just like you did. We'll get involved in issues,
environmental stuff. We're going to hand out leaflets,
tack up posters and knock on doors
just like you did and protect the planet."
Ralph nodded in his eager puppy way, hunger for acceptance
transcending politics. "Without you we'd never have thought
of it. Now we'll be part of the process, not just hanging out.
We wanted you to know first." Justin gave Ralph a friendly
shove. "Oh yeah," Ralph said. "We wanted to say thanks."
Justin smiled like he'd delivered a straight "A" report card.
"All that commune stuff you told us about, the self
sufficiency, being into the land and all that, I mean
those dudes had their heads in the right place
even if they couldn't quite get it together."

My face reflected the boys' contagious smiles as I got a sweet
whiff of how promising the world once seemed and imagined
them breathing that same air. Self sufficiency's romance
was an aphrodisiac. Maybe we'd finally keep the promises
we made to ourselves. Was I at last making a difference,
the old stories of failed aspiration becoming more
than fireside fairy tales by inspiring the kids?
Perhaps my generation's exploits weren't destined to change
the world then, but to awaken the future. I was opening
in a way I hadn't expected. "We want to help in the garden,"
Justin insisted. "And hear one of those cross-country stories,"
Ralph added, his voice rising at the end to a question mark.
"Sure," I said. "Who are you campaigning for?"
Justin reached for the pitchfork standing upright in front
of me. "My dad's running for first selectman.
Says he wants to give the land a voice. The environment
is one of his big things. Isn't that cool?
Dude, I'll bet we'll be campaigning right here at the dump."

My stomach knotted and my face must have dropped
as Justin's sudden concerned look became a question
about my health. Muttering something about a sore back,
I walked to the shed returning with a second pitchfork

and a rake. "You guys turn over the soil
and I'll crush the clods so the dirt's fine and soft,
especially where carrots and other root crops will be seeded."
With a nod they set to work. "Could we hear more about
the commune?" My mind raced for the right story.
Mickey Lamb was up to something and I had to watch myself.
No more tales with drugs or nudity. "Okay,
but this one's about a very different kind of place.
The world wasn't all hippy dippy type stuff."

*Heading back east near the trip's end, I got dropped
in Denver by a young farmer type in a rusty flatbed pickup
hauling a load of manure down to Colorado Springs. Thumb
out, I stood on the Federal Avenue ramp to I-70 about two
hours without anyone so much as looking at me, though traffic
was thick. It was getting dark, the Front Range
growing slowly to an ominous charcoal wall, lights
coming on in the flatlands to the east. But I wasn't worried
because one of the lifeline phone numbers Frodo
had given me before I left Drop was for a Denver
cat named Pisces who had a place with plenty
of room to crash. Slinging the pack over my shoulder
I marched into the city, finding a phone booth in a pharmacy.*

*A second ring and I was suddenly cut off. Static and a stilted
female voice announced that the number was no longer
in service. My dime pinged into the coin return
and I tried again, getting the same cranky old-woman voice
of boredom and annoyance. Maybe I'd jotted the number
wrong, but I couldn't very well dial information
for a Mr. Pisces. In the middle of Denver fucking Colorado
and surrounded by millions, I felt alone for the first time
in weeks of travel. My head throbbed with hunger.
It looked like rain.*

*I thought of a night in the slammer, but getting arrested
wasn't so easy with no cops around and I was too chicken
to get caught stealing or throwing a rock through a window.*

*Besides, the Mayberry jail cell in Andy Griffith
where you might get locked in with some genial drunk
was just a lie. Dangerous people were behind bars in big
cities. I got directions and headed to the railroad
station thinking I might sleep on a bench or in a bathroom
stall. Fortunately, they turned out wrong. I found myself
walking through a strange daylight of brightly lit signs
rooting for car dealerships, gas stations,
and fast food joints, eventually arriving in a neighborhood
of small stores and corner bars that soon became a street
of big houses down on their uppers, once fashionable places
divided into apartments or offices. Here I spotted a large,
hand painted orange and yellow sign
in the form of a smiling sun. Bright incandescence poured
from the windows. "Sunshine House," read the big block
letters. "All Are Welcome." I knocked on the door.*

A NIGHT WITH JESUS

"So, I was right. It was another commune,"
Ralph said, picking up a stone
and sidearming it into a thicket of raspberry canes.
"Sort of but, no, not really."
"A youth hostel," Justin suggested, though reading my face
he quickly switched his vote to soup kitchen.
"In a way it was like all three, but not exactly."
Ralph turned over another forkful of soil.
"But you were able to bum a free meal, weren't you?"
I nodded. "Left with a full belly and laid out no cash,
but it wasn't exactly free." Justin looked puzzled.
"Lots of worms here," he said, reaching for a night crawler.

Tapping on an aluminum screen door, I peered into a dimly
lit hallway with thick dark wood moldings. I rattled the door
with a second knock. From out of shadows at the far end
came squeaking floorboards and lively steps.
A smiling face with close cropped curly hair opened
the door and extended a hand. Staring me right in the eyes,
he shook my hand firmly, his cheeks puffed
with smile like a squirrel face filled with nuts.

"Call me Julian, my bother. Come in and lay your burden
down," he said, gazing at the pack. "I'm sure your travels

have been hard." He had a long crooked nose,
wore a pink oxford cloth shirt and dark new jeans a couple
sizes too big. Leading me down a hall, he recited rules
in a fatherly tone though maybe he was twenty-three.
No drinking, smoking or woman guests and I could stay
up to three nights by participating in Bible readings.
We passed a couple closed doors and then a parlor
with a dozen people propped on pillows while talking.
It smelled of old newspapers and furniture polish.
A swinging leather door with big brass nail heads led
to a kitchen awash in florescence where white
enamel cabinets glowed. "I'm sorry we've already shared
the evening meal," Julian said, "but sit yourself down,
brother. You look weak. Such as we have, you shall have."

"Is this some kind of church?" I asked, remembering a TV
newsclip I'd seen about a Catholic home for runaways.
"Only in Saint Paul's sense—a group banded together
serving Jesus." Julian went to grab some grub
while I sat at a small Formica table alongside a night
darkened window reflecting the room. The light behind
me caused a glow around my head like an angel
in a medieval painting. It gave me the creeps.

Julian returned with a chipped china bowl of steaming stew,
a thick slice of black bread, a glass of water
and that unquenchable smile that seemed to extend his Mickey
Mouse ears. "Enjoy the repast, brother. I'll return shortly."
From down the hallway I heard soft singing
and guitar strumming. Drop City gone straight and pious?

Music had ended when Julian returned
as I soaked up the last bit of stew with bread.
"Almost 9:15," he said, with a wristwatch glance,
"and it's lights out by ten so let me show you to the shower
and bunks." The constant professional smile set me on edge,
like bright headlights tailgating on an unlit road.
In a basement with green linoleum floors and gray painted

brick walls that smelled like a YMCA locker
room, he showed me the shower and I tossed my pack
onto a springy bunk. The water was warm and welcoming.

Wrapped in a towel, I came out of the shower
to find a big guy with pasty black hair and a hint of mustache
stretched out on one of the other bunks. Frank
was vagabonding his way around the country going from soup
kitchen to construction job and taking off when he felt
like it, a kind of throwback to Woody Guthrie
hobo days. "Thank God you're not full of all that smiley
'brother' shit," he said with a broad grin.
"Of course, can't be too careful. Might have baptized
you with that shower." We laughed and dowsed the lights.

"So they were Jesus freaks," Ralph said, hauling
a wheelbarrow from the compost pile.
"Could call 'em that. They definitely had a mission."
I turned to Justin. "Hold the screen.
Ralph's going to put a shovelful of compost
onto it. Shake until the fines fall through, then toss the big
stuff into that bucket. Garden waste and food
scraps coming back as rich soil. The only time you'll really
get something for nothing." I turned back to Ralph.
"At Sunshine House you didn't have to whip out your wallet,
but they made you pay. Beware of people with an agenda
who are in love with an idea or a slogan, a campaign."
I thought of Mickey Lamb, newly chameleon green,
and hoped I hadn't come down too heavy on the boys.

WORMS IN THE GARDEN

*I awakened to a high pitched whistle penetrating a dream,
the soft green radium dial of my watch glowing 5:07.
Rubbing my eyes, I focused on a goateed guy in clean
white sneakers fingering a recorder and standing
in the doorway like some magical elf playing one of those soft,
annoying storybook shepherd tunes. Frank hadn't stirred,
a lump wrapped in a chrysalis of brown blanket.
The elf began playing Greensleeves, and when I looked back
he was gone, the melody wafting down the stairway
and slowly fading. "Shit! Is tutti flutti gone yet?"
rasped a voice from under the covers. "How can
they be so damn full of religion at this ungodly hour?"*

*Laughter and conversation buzzed from the dining room
and we entered as our musical alarm clock
was setting the table, a long wooden thing that might
have been a refugee from a bankrupt
corporate board room. It was as dark as the moldings
around the room's wide entryway though sunlight poured
like syrup through the tall windows and made it glow.
We sat and suddenly silence reigned, everyone bent in prayer.*

*"Lord," Julian began solemnly, "bless this meal
and this house serving you. Give us strength
to proceed with your good work." He paused,*

*and I looked up like it was over, but he continued.
"Especially look after our guests, that they may be safe
from harm, for in their own way they too are here to serve
you." Like a bobble-head doll I looked up again, but Julian
went on. "Peace be unto this house and our brothers
and sisters called on distant errands." A collective "amen"
arose as if from a deep well.*

*Sausage, scrambled eggs, cereal, toast and coffee cake
were passed around amidst eruptions of lively conversation.
Julian introduced everyone by name. They talked biblical
passages and Tom Seaver's fastball like a frat house
with God's Good Housekeeping Seal. Swarthy Matthew,
wearing a plastic pocket protector stuffed with pens,
sat on my left and struck up a conversation with the usual
where's and whys. He worked in a supermarket and often
swung by for breakfast and morning prayer.
A burly blond house member asked for the salt.
"But if the salt have lost its savor, wherewith
shall it be salted?" Matthew asked, passing the shaker
to Seymour who winked and laughed.*

*Frank ate heartily, surrounded by a sullen bubble,
speaking like a monosyllabic teen only when spoken
to, determined not to surrender any satisfaction of being
reachable. Maybe it was far-offness from home,
the intoxication of a good meal and strong coffee,
or ingrained manners, but I replied to Matthew's welcome
mat manner and he didn't hesitate to seize the moment.
"In the end," he concluded, "your mom didn't stand
in your way, and your father will feel the presence
of your effort. Both are expressions of love that will heal
the rifts of divorce and distance."
I shook my head and responded more for punctuation
than in understanding. "Well, maybe."*

*"Trust me brother," Matthew almost whispered,
"it wasn't until I met Jesus that I found sufficient love*

*for all. With his help you, too, will find relationships
growing in harmony."* Suddenly I was naked,
vulnerable to his practiced good will.
I felt conned into confessing, suckered by a sales pitch.

Looking around the room as if for the first time,
it seemed as if all these people wore a uniform,
cultivating endless smiles, an occupational friendliness
regardless of what was said. I felt watched,
judged, as if they were parents. Maybe folks at Drop City
had a kind of uniform—long hair, army jackets, worn jeans.
Still, they didn't all seem robotically the same, and everyone
did their own thing without laying down a big trip.

Brother Gregory, the recorder player, began clearing dishes.
Others pitched in and some went to the kitchen putting away
food, washing and drying. Unlike Drop, there was clearly
a schedule. Sink-bound with a load of plates,
I turned to Julian as he wiped the table.
"I just wanted to say thanks. Super meal."
Vacantly sparkling eyes seemed to penetrate my skull.
"Silver and gold have I none, but such as I have I give thee."
He put a palm on my shoulder.
"Please join us for bible study," he added.

Lacking chairs, we sat in a circle on a worn Persian
rug in an old fashioned parlor. Almost empty bookcases
lined one wall and an upright piano occupied a corner.
Seymour handed out note cards with handwritten
biblical phrases. At his request, I was the first to read aloud
what was written. Despite a size and brawn
that made him seem more natural changing crankcase oil
or working behind a butcher's counter, Seymour
shared the soft voice and annoyingly angelic smile
of the others. "For none of us liveth to himself
and no man dieth to himself. Romans 14:7," I read.

*"And for you, my brother," Seymour asked, "what wisdom
does this hold?" Surveying the calmly smiling faces
so estranged from Sandoz's Cheshire cat grin,
I found Frank's smirk of boredom and resentment an oasis.
A discussion about the brotherhood of man blew
up like a squall and I felt clever remembering my tenth grade
homeroom teacher's coffee mug quoting John Donne's
"no man is an island." But, my thoughts were orphaned
and whatever was said somehow devolved
into finding connection by living and dying in Christ.*

*"Out of the abundance of the heart the mouth speaketh,"
Frank read with flat-voiced boredom. With shoulder shrugs
he deflected questions like a hockey goalie defending
the net. They treated him with sick-puppy pity, but the looks
of concern seemed aimed like arrows, the discussion fired
in a fusillade of comments, one marching after another,
charging like a military assault. Freaky
how everything got twisted toward foregone
conclusions. Mistaking my civility for consent,
they saw acceptance though I felt adrift.
For the first time I wanted out of a group.*

*Crazed after all five cards were read, I hustled
to the basement to pack my gear, as Frank walked
out the front door without a word, though his kit was laid
out like he was planning on another night. Frank was strong,
impenetrable, impossible to bludgeon,
but I couldn't hack the hassle and bullshit.*

*"Every man shall bear his own burden,"
pronounced Julian, standing at the top of the stairs
and looking over my pack, his eyes beating
down like sunlamps. "Are you leaving us?"
I shook my head. "Guess I'm restless. So much to see.
Not sure I fit in exactly, but everyone was real nice."
Hallway hardwood creaked as I headed toward the door.*

"Well many are called, but few are chosen,"
he said, looking at me with sad concern. In his pupils
I saw nothing but my own reflection. How I wanted to laugh
at that smile, make him angry, have him curse me. "The Lord
be with you," he said gently, almost mechanically,
squeezing my forearm as I opened the screen door.

"Dude, like you were lucky to back away from those holy
rollers without more trouble," Ralph said, sliding
another shovelful of compost onto the screen. "It sounded
like zombie-think, telling you what to believe and all."
Justin sifted and new soil, dark and fine as ground coffee
drifted downward, orange peel and eggshell fragments
and a couple of pebbles caught and tossed away.
Putting down the screen, he pulled his iPhone
from his pocket. "It's getting late," he said to Ralph.
"We gotta get going. Don't worry," he added, turning
to me, "we'll be back soon to help. And we'll see a lot
of each other once the campaign heats up 'cause Dad
says he wants to press the flesh at the dump."

GHOST REDUX

Déjà vu all over again, the ghosts seemed to enter whatever
void the boys had left, as if their presence
had precipitated a residue or created a kind of slow-to-fill
vacuum or magnetic field. With Star Trek fantasies,
I saw their words floating around me, reforming into new
phrases and sentences, song snippets, headlines
and lightning flash verbiage long gone from the lexicon.
My storytelling was gravitational, pulling words
from the past's black hole, liberating decades
old utterances to roam the present.

BIAFRANS FACE A NEW WAVE OF STARVATION

Heliotrope, an independent free university in San Francisco,
offers courses in body surfing howling at the moon and bofing

NATIONS BEGINNING TO CONSIDER
WHO OWNS WHAT ON THE MOON

BIRTH CONTOL UNIT TO AID ADOLESCENTS

Worried about student protests, the University
of California at Los Angeles took the unusual step
of bestowing honorary degrees in private.

ENEMY BELIEVED TO AIM AT CONTROL
OF COUNTRYSIDE

Your Next Car: The Great New Chrysler

GOVERNMENT WARNING

Sunday mornings while others slept or readied for church
and the dump was closed, I sat in my American dream
Airstream office, the silver bullet of middle class
vacations, pouring over invoices, email, the carting company
schedules of pick up and drop off, evaluating
the need for rolloffs and recycling containers, making sure
manifests for hazmat and e-waste were in order.
I banged at my keyboard until Congregationalists
called their flock with bombilating bells
at ten o'clock and then played the recorded
carillon ringing with "America" and "Ode to Joy."

I delight in measuring society's waste,
a kind of schadenfreude for a world run amuck,
though I'd never admit it. This bubble of gleaming stainless
with the propane heater roaring in winter and summer's air
conditioned hum is my house of worship where I momentarily
lose myself in the purity of calculations and abstract figures.
Secure in the locked gate of Sunday solitude, I revel
in my shining refuge surrounded outside
by serendipitous prizes of my labor, a satirical gauntlet
of garden gnomes and whirligigs, an old wagon wheel, broken
bicycle lacking handlebars, a rusting slant-six-Chevy engine,
a pile of composting elephant dung

from last year's Barnum and Bailey visit to Hartford,
a mannequin in torn lacy lingerie, a six foot wooden hot dog
once on the roof of a demolished stand that fed
Route 44 travelers from the fifties to the eighties,
and by the steps, two toilets, one avocado, one pink.

Expecting church bells tolling, I startled to a soft tap
and then an impatient rapping at the door, a shock
with the gate locked. At first I thought it might be the boys,
yet unlikely so early on Sunday. But with soil still moist
from Justin's forking, I conjured Mickey Lamb, his face
flushed and contorted, carrying anger like a heavy tool chest.
Even through the door I felt chilled in the shadow
of his brawny high school wrestler build.
I hesitated. The knock grew louder, more insistent
as I looked around the room for a pipewrench or knife
to defend myself. As I reached for a broken mop handle,
a high pitched woman's voice shouted in a tone usually
reserved for telling a child to clean his room a third time:
"Will you come to the damn door already, Caleb.
I can see your shadow on the window shade."
The broom handle clattered to the linoleum floor.
"It's unlocked," I replied.

"What the hell, Caleb," Beryl Proulx said, shaking her head
as she opened the door. I gave an exaggerated bow
to my old friend from grammar school days.
"And for what do I owe the honor of a visit
from the esteemed first select*woman*?"
Beryl slammed the door and stood hands on hips, tall
and elegant even in jeans and a sweatshirt, like a stunt double
for Meryl Streep. "How many times have I told you it's
select*man*. That's what the charter says and that's what it is.
Don't try to impress me with your gender sensitivity.
I've known you too long. And can't you clean
up a bit. This is a town office and it looks
like a derelict's tag sale out there."

"It's a highly selective collection appropriate
to the location that enables us to look at ordinary
stuff as objects d' art. I merely want to meet state
requirements for public art in government institutions."
She shook her head. "And the toilets?"
I raised an instructive finger. "My outdoor conference room.
Colored porcelain is easier to keep clean."
With a sigh of cheerful exasperation she asked, "Could you
at least do something about the dummy?"
I raised an eyebrow. "You think the black lace is too much?
Maybe I misjudged the cup size, but it's all I had.
You got anything you don't need anymore?"
She sat and crossed her long legs in the only other chair
in the room, a once classy dining piece that, without a back,
was now a kind of stool. "Seriously, that car engine
has got to be worth something for scrap."
I grinned. "Been here since Billy Bartley's day. It'd be
sacrilege to move." She rolled her long lashed hazel eyes.
"A bit heavy, too, I imagine."

"So, on a Sunday you come to argue about my art collection?"
"I need to speak with you privately."
"About art?"
"No, about the kids who've been hanging out around here."
"Since when is a dump not wholesome enough?
 Our dads let us run on the burning pile looking for treasures.
I built a go-cart with the stuff I found."
"You know very well it's about your stories,
Caleb. Some of the parents are complaining."
"Who has a problem?"
"It doesn't matter."
"Of course it does. You've been in politics long
enough to know you don't buy what every wing-nut
is selling. It was Mickey Lamb, wasn't it."
"I heard about the Third Base scuffle, but it's not just him
and it's not just about the boys who've been here.
Kids talk, word gets around, things get blown
out of proportion. I've got parents complaining

because they think you're the reason their kids
are downloading drug lyrics. Another doesn't like the tie-dye
his kid is wearing, and Chief Aarons
says a couple of them were caught hitchhiking."

"Well whoop-de-do! I'm just telling it like was, and I'm even
leaving out the worst of the sex, drugs and rock-and-roll—
which were never as good as legend would have it anyway.
Last time, I even told them about a Christian commune
I crashed. How can there be complaints about that?"
"It's not even what you say,
it's what these parents think you are saying."
"The kids were interested before they climbed the fence."
"Of course they were. I'm not here to argue.
I just want to warn you what's going down, that's all."
"This is a public place and they're entitled to be here.
I got hired years ago 'cause I'm honest. You want me to lie?"
"Just tone it down a little, that's all."
"It's really about politics, isn't it? You're worried Lamb
will kick your ass in the election. Just cut me loose,
let me twist in the wind. I can handle it."
"Look," Beryl said, her voice rising slightly
as her politician's cool faded, "I'm sticking by you.
I've had your back so long you don't even know it. It's you
who's going to get hurt," she said getting up. "Just
give it some thought," she continued, opening the door
to peeling church bells.

BACK TO THE GARDEN

I knew they'd be back hungry for stories,
and little more than a week proved right. I wrestled
with what to tell them, hardly cowed, instead tempted to push
back at intimidation and feed their new found
fascination with politics by spinning tales
about swimming in the Reflecting Pool
and shouting obscenities at the White House
in the exhilarated crowds of the 1971 Moratorium:
"One, two, three, four, Tricky Dick stop the war!"
I'd tell them how I was boosted
to sit in Lincoln's lap, a more powerful political act
than campaigning for a first selectman candidate.
If they wanted to get something done for the environment,
maybe they should sit in big trees,
throw themselves in front of Mickey Lamb's bulldozers.

I wasn't going to knuckle under and buckle down,
so maybe I'd spill stories of wild Dionysian revels
shaking to the twin drummer heartbeat of a Dead concert
where the air was clouded with hash and reefer
smoke and barefooted guys and chicks danced wildly,
playing hackysack with their feet until dropping in ecstatic
exhaustion. A passive aggressive barrage, perhaps,
but I'd send a message to Mickey Lamb and his minions.
I'd tell of dropping acid on the Appalachian

Trail at Numeral Rock where kids from Kent School
painted their class colors on a ledge caked with years
of cracked and flaking paint. In the year of the "class
with the bad attitude," my friend Jacki and I watched the sun
play on the spruce and hemlock slopes of Schaghticoke Mountain where real Indians
still roamed. Amped reflections
in bent rainbow shapes rose in waves off the broad
Housatonic winding through fields patched green
and amber with grain. I'd tell them about the pulsing flashes
of color, the wired electric hum and giddy endless grin
that made me seem more than myself.
Stories to entangle Lamb like barbed wire.

As always, high on the smell of damp spring soil and tempted
to plant before the time of the season, I itched for three
p.m. when I latched the gate and headed for the garden
on the gamble of a good forecast, Memorial Day still a week
away. Bending over makeshift cold frames, I moved tender
plants with the delicacy of glass, the glossy leaved peppers,
the dusty-green miniature eggplant, and tomatoes,
some with tiny yellow flower bells among the deeply indented
and intricate greenery. Raking out the soil until fine
and almost sand-like, I'd lined up the tiny plants
in orderly rows like childhood's toy soldiers when Justin,
Ralph, Billy and Ronny arrived, Ronny behind the wheel
of his mom's Honda. "You're just
in time to get things in the ground," I said.

Returning with tools from the shed, I showed them the proper
planting depth and two boys set out with trowels
as I followed, placing seedlings in the holes. Behind
me Justin was sprinkling sifted compost and Billy
tipped a watering can. Bursting with talk about campaigning
like most boys buzz about cars or girls, I was heartened
that my McCarthy tales had led to bigger
things, though the taint of Mickey Lamb tempered
my enthusiasm. Ronny, who hoped to be a tattoo artist
and spent time drawing Escher-like designs

when he should have been taking notes in class,
was designing an online brochure for email blasts.
They planned to hold a voter registration drive at school,
and were making lists of places to put up posters and hand
out leaflets. If Beryl were beat, credit the boys, not Mickey
Lamb's charm or positions. And barely a row planted,
they wanted a trip story so I chose one from a time
when Vietnam was the continental divide of campaigns.

*Heading home and beat after too many miles, too little sleep
and irregular meals, I was eager for the breakfast table
and bed I'd known since forever, surprisingly hungry
for the dull familiar faces and boring daily routines. Pumped
to soon hit Pennsylvania and wide awake, dosed on adrenalin
from a rocking, teeth chattering tractor-trailer ride
with a load of steel rods on I-80 from Toledo to Youngstown
past mills and pavement, smokestacks, railroad tracks,
transmission lines, towers of fifty-five gallon drums and piles
of junk cars, I flagged a ride and crammed
into a small, but muscular '67 Mustang.*

*A mustache nestled like a caterpillar below the driver's nose,
his bulging cheeks were bluish with five o'clock shadow
and brown eyes sunk into deep socket hollows beneath a head
of thick black hair. Dark curls spewed from the neck
of a chambray work shirt and a pack of cigarettes bulged
from each pocket. Bell bottoms too short revealed big black
army boots. "Yeah, I was a fucking soldier," the driver
said catching my stare. "Got hit in the leg and blew
my fucking knee apart. But doctors are fucking geniuses
and now I got all these Humpty Dumpty pieces
in me. I'm part fucking robot."*

*"Almost worth it, getting sent stateside, I mean. Purple Heart
though ain't worth shit on a shingle. People don't know
whether to treat you like a hero or criminal, sos they don't say
nothing. The fucking pits, man. Other vets look
at you like Nam wasn't a real war, you know, not like the big*

*one, dubya dubya two. I'm sure as shit glad to be outta
there with guys making believe their firing rounds, nervous
Nellies who'll shoot at the slightest noise, and those gung ho
types who love nothin' more than snuffin' Gooks.
So much bullshit going down, man, with bugs as big
as your hand and stewing in your own sweat.
You wouldn't believe the size of the rats, man.*

It was like he wasn't even talking to me, just coughing
up this phlegm of feeling caught in his throat.
"Got Nebraska plates, I see." He nodded.
"Yeah, from the Sand Hills out west. George Crabber's
the name," he said, extending his hand.
"Got home 'bout six fucking months ago and my old lady
she seemed kind of out of it and I thought she was pissed
'cause I'm still having these crazy fucking sweaty screaming
dreams hearing mortar fire and seeing the faces of guys
that don't exist no more. Turns out that while I'm doing my
tour she got tight with some bartender from down Ogallala
way. I come home to find a note on the six pack in the fridge
and the next day a sheriff's fucking delivering papers.

"After a couple weeks of deep alone I took up with my folks
twenty miles down the road. Just about begged
me to come home and then Dad and I got into fucking fights
'cause he thinks we ought to drop an A-bomb on Hanoi
or something, and man, I'm like just get the hell
out. Two days ago he says I gotta get a better job
than doing farm labor 'cause I'm not putting enough into
the food bill. Says I wasn't man enough to hold
on to my fucking old lady. Winds up hitting me. First time
since I was kid. Before I know it, I slug him right across
the jaw like some Saigon bar fight. I mean I never hit
him before and I can't even say how it happened.
So I just up and left, fucking drove around like a drunk
though cold sober. Going to see my brother
doing some hippie shit in Burlington, Vermont.
Never got along that good as kids, but I think

he gets this crap." George stole a glance at the dash.
"*Holy shit! Gotta get some gas. Next exit and we're good.*"

He spoke slowly, deliberately, but something almost
frightening in his voice gripped me—like he might go postal
any minute. In his depth of pain, his horror, the trivialities
of my life seemed to melt. I felt guilty about the starry-night-
bonfire-anti-war-vigils burning on UConn hillsides
where uniforms went up in flames, and about my plans
to toast my card and head north of the border
when my number came up. There was collateral damage
I didn't even have a hint about. Just to make conversation,
I asked when he'd filled up last, what he got for gas
mileage. What else could I say? He didn't seem to hear.

Parking lot pavement broken and spotted with oil, a giant red
Pegasus trademark was perched on the roof of the battered
Mobil station like Santa's sleigh. An older man in a green
uniform and a tightly fitted Pittsburgh Pirates
cap with the bill backward came to the window.
"*What'll it be?*" *He seemed to talk through his nose.*
"*Fill'er,*" *George said. "All righty.*"
Opening the door, George turned to me. "Gotta
take a fucking wicked leak. Be right back."
Moving slowly across the pavement with an awkward
limp, as if one leg were a bit shorter than the other,
he didn't need a purple heart to prove anything.

George returned as the attendant with kindly grandfather
eyes and hands creased with grease finished the windows.
The newly discharged vet grimaced as he walked back,
but it didn't seem so much pain as force of effort knotting
his face. He seemed to limp from so many things.
The old man stared at George's awkward gait and quickly
turned his head when George looked up, searching
his pockets for cash. "That'll be seven even," *the old man*
croaked, as George peeled off the bills. "Thanks a lot, boys,"
he called, as the ex-soldier got into the car, "thanks a lot."

Boys. Boys. Boys. Couldn't the old fart
see what the man had been through?
The word pounded inside me like a headache.

Pulling out with tires squealing, he drove back
to the interstate like we were being chased. An eight cylinder,
it had enough horses to easily hit the century mark on the big
road. He kept it to about seventy-five and the tiny towns
among hilly woods flashed past. "You want to come north
with me? George asked as we zoomed by a sign
for Berwick. "I'm gonna cruise up ol' I-81 to Binghamton
and cut fucking east to the Catskills
and crash at a place called Woodstock.
There's a fucking big outdoor concert happening on some
dairy farm out there. You interested?"

"Sounds really far-out, but I don't know. I've been bumming
around for weeks and thinking of heading home. I'm getting
tired of the whole scene. Kinda burned out."
George gave a low whistle from between his teeth.
"There's s'posed to be some real outta sight groups: Country
Joe, Joni Mitchell, Hendrix, Steve Stills and a whole fucking
bunch I can't remember." I shook my head.
"Sounds real tempting."
He slapped his thigh. "You betcha! I heard Dylan lives
around there somewhere. No telling but he might show up."
"You think so."
"Why the fuck else would they hold it so fucking close by?"

Darkness grew like a cataract over the lens of the day
as we passed the dead end coal piles of Wilkes Barre
and Scranton, lights coming on in the hills like terrestrial
stars. Entering New York, he took 17 west, a wide curving
road with grades that worked the engine. The car
took the terrain like a tiger chasing prey. Route 30 was next,
a narrow snaking road following river
bends weaving through a valley the river had carved.

I'm not sure exactly when we hit traffic,
but suddenly it seemed we were crawling
along slowly, exhaust thick in the heat. Finally, the cars
just stopped and the road became a parking lot. Lights
doused, people got out and started walking, a real freak
parade of tie dye, headbands, peasant blouses and frayed
faded jeans along with armloads of blankets,
tarps and bags of food. With engines idle, the sweet incense
of reefer floated in the air and I breathed deeply.
George grabbed a bedroll and flashlight
out of the back seat. "Roget's Thesaurus devotes
seventy-eight lines to 'peace' and 162 to 'warfare,'"
he said, slamming the Mustang's door.
"I know. I've had time to count them." We shook hands,
and after a teetering hesitancy, embraced.
He went with the flow
as I unknowingly walked away from the pivotal
event of my generation, never to see him again.

Suddenly I awoke as if from a trance, the boys
standing around me seemingly high on the same hypnosis,
the planting barely half done and me unsure
how long we'd been mesmerized.
"Let's get the rest of these seedlings in the ground,"
I said, at last breaking the spell.
"I thought you were at Woodstock,"
Billy said as he bent his muscular body and placed a tiny
tomato plant in the soil. "That's what everyone says."
"I heard it from a bunch of people—even Justin's dad."
I laughed. "That tells you something, doesn't it?"
Justin spilled some compost around a plant.
"For us, saving the environment is like ending the war
was to you. And people are getting hurt just like that vet,
but instead of bullets its poisoned water and air, cancer
and birth defects. My dad is going to help fix
that. Can we hand out leaflets at the dump?
It'll be just like you did, standing on street corners
and at factory gates for McCarthy." I felt a lump in the pit
of my stomach. "It's a free country," was all I could manage.

GHOSTS RETURNING

The images came without warning
    like unexpectedly encountering a friend from years past,
    words erupting and exploding in visions long forgotten—
the old fast food hangouts, the deep woods
now a subdivision, the feral dog roaming an empty lot,
the way a buddy's mom spoke with an Italian accent,
or the D-cup girls who sunbathed
nude on the roof next door thinking themselves unseen.
One conjured headline or ad led to another
connecting adventures hidden years ago,
out of focus photos of past recollections
in a dusty attic trunk. New was old and old was new.

PIPELINE PLANNED TO TAP ARCTIC GAS

By any measure, this electronically amplified paean
to peace pot and permissiveness called "Hair"
is the "My Fair Lady" of the now generation

INVER HOUSE SCOTCH: SOFT AS A KISS

It's written in the ashes of the village towns we've burned

RALLY HELD TO OPPOSE ABM

Larry Poland of Miami Bible College complained
that the Apollo 10 astronauts carried the "language
of the street" to the moon and called on the crew
to repent their "profanity, vulgarity and blasphemy"

PENTAGON FACES SUIT ON GRAPES, CHAVEZ AND

TOWN MEETING

Next I saw the boys, they stood beside the garbage compactor
or guarded the recycling rolloff handing out leaflets
with Lamb's toothy grin, his nomination by Democrats
without much caucus grumbling, I heard.
Smiling, they helped lift trash from the back of pickups
and trunks of cars, tossed bundled papers and bottles
into the new single stream system
ensuring everyone left with the handbill detailing Lamb
as a four-letter-sport product of local schools
and as a contractor building small subdivisions and strip
shopping plazas, not so much to nail down a paycheck,
but create jobs in his community. There was some vague
pabulum about supporting schools and new athletic fields
and saving the environment, the last catching in the craw
of my conscience, remembering from not too many
years ago his bulldozers breaking silt fences, filling wetlands,
paving bog turtle and Jefferson salamander
habitat with the sheepish excuse that his workmen goofed.
It wasn't the first time and wouldn't be the last.

My tomatoes grew tall and popped gold star flowers,
eggplants knee high with pendant buds and peppers stretching
to the light, but the boys were blind to this miracle of soil
and sun, besotted with politics as they proudly did their duty

for the planet after school and on Saturdays, confident
that Lamb's election would clean up the environment
and greeting me cheerfully for birthing their sense of mission,
their stake in the world's fate. I'd given them a power
they wore in the way they walked. How to explain
that aching appetite for stories become loaves and fishes
sustaining them, but leaving the storyteller famished?
Yet their questions had breathed life into me, allowed
me to relive reveries I thought long past, an embarrassing
world of "far-out" and "trippy" doings
I had dismissed and forced to disappear in time and spirit.
Now I was on the cusp of discarding the psychedelic noise
and tie dye trappings, recovering, recycling
my past into something useful that made my life seem larger,
at last connected. Their enthusiasm finally gave me words,
a voice for a time and place once discarded as junk,
a way to reap a cosmic profit. I needed their energy
to rediscover myself, to find stories that seemed paralyzed,
aimless without an audience. I felt as if I'd lost
an engrossing novel I was reading just at the book's midpoint.

Wallowing in my back pages, I got a heads-up call
from Beryl, the usual friendly tease drained from her voice.
Lamb was making a major announcement,
using the selectmen's meeting to broadcast his campaign
promise to close the landfill as an environmental
insult and hazard to health. She didn't want me caught
in the political crossfire, but needed me for facts and figures.
There would be a lot of verbal garbage being dumped
in the room, subject to my disposal. She'd tried to keep
it off the agenda, but was a lone Republican
sandwiched between two Democrats, old cronies of Lamb
who wanted him in the top job, and it was hard to refuse
listening to a new idea. So a week after schools closed
for summer and my garden was a riot of green
with squash snaking over the plot at inches
a day and my asparagus gone to feathery ferns,
I made my way up the broad brownstone steps of town hall.

Imposingly urban for a rural town, the small building
of incongruously heavy sandstone blocks and brick
with its riot of gables, twin spires and Spanish tile roof
had a deep arching entrance suggesting the mouth of a cave.
Today the town could ill afford to keep it in repair,
let alone construct such a grand structure, but at the turn
of the twentieth century it had been a gift of Micah Belcher,
president of the button factory then booming
at the falls of the Seven Mile River at the edge
of Westmoreland village. Today the sprawling redbrick mill
sat largely vacant but for storage and an auto body shop.

Beryl had just gaveled the hearing room to a silence
that seemed to echo from its hardwood floors and oak
wainscoting. The place was packed with about fifty people,
all of whom knew each other, most sporting Lamb buttons.
"First on our agenda," Beryl said in a voice unusually brittle,
"is our public forum, and I recognize Mickey Lamb
for a presentation." With his ex-wrestler's physique,
Lamb stood like a pillar supporting the building,
and with muscular confidence gave the customary
thank-yous and acknowledgements.

"When I have the honor of election to this town's highest
office," he began with a sweep of his hand around the room,
his sapphire blue eyes seeming to burn
through you as he looked from face to face,
"I propose to close the landfill and turn it into a park.
At a height of over 500 feet, 140 above this very room,
it will command a fine view of the river
and this village. I envision a road and bike
path winding to the top where there'll be a gazebo
with binocular posts. It will be a hot spot for weddings
and birthday parties, and a reasonable charge
will help recoup the cost of construction and maintenance.
On the lower, more level slopes where the office,
superintendent's cottage and rolloff containers now stand,

we'll build ballfields for our children. We could even
put in a bunny-slope rope tow for winter skiing.
I think we can accommodate a dog park." As Lamb's voice
dropped in conclusion, applause chattered through the room.

"A nice idea, Mr. Lamb," Beryl responded, trying to break
the magnetism of the mood, "but the taxpayers
of this town can hardly keep pace with funding our current
parks and fields. And combing through the numbers
provided by Sanitary Landfill Superintendent Dempster,
comparing nearby communities, I'm convinced the cost
of running the landfill is much cheaper than hauling
trash to an energy recovery incinerator."
Lamb rocked back on his heels, seemed like a fighter
prepared to pounce on an opponents mistaken move.

"With all due respect madam first selectwoman,"
Lamb replied with overly polite condescension,
"first of all, a report I had commissioned," he said, waving
a binder of papers, "indicates substantial revenues
from landfill gas recovery and an array of solar panels
which I intend to propose. It will make us a leader
in green energy spurring further economic development.
But more important, I don't think the small amount of savings
is worth this dump's health risk and threat to the Seven
Mile River. Do we really want to be known
as Connecticut's dump town, last of the dinosaurs?"
A murmur rolled through the crowd.
"Go for it, Mick!" someone shouted.
"The people here deserve better," Lamb continued. "No,
they demand better and have a right to it. Rainwater
filters and infiltrates this hideous hill of garbage
producing a toxic and noxious brew that may be laced
with toluene and xylene, phenols and cresols, benzene,
cadmium and methyl naphthalene. There's mercury
and nickel, lead, alkanes and phenols—
and that's just from normal household garbage.
Who knows what witches' stew of chemicals were buried

before anyone knew better in the days of Belcher Button—
cutting oils and degreasers, plating fluids, at the very least.
The plume spills right into the Seven Mile,
our greatest natural resource where our kids swim, fish
and paddle their canoes. We can't afford to keep the dump.
The day is long past when the solution to pollution
was dilution." A cloudburst of applause swept across
the room leaving Beryl looking sunken and alone.

Bloated with steroidal rhetoric, Lamb went on like a fire
and brimstone preacher, stretching the truth, spicing
it with a white lie, playing on fears for children
and community pride while Beryl shot glances
my way. I hoped she wouldn't call on me, but she almost
had no choice. I wanted to help, but the mood of the crowd
seemed beyond redemption. How did a child of the sixties
come to defend this abscess on the face of the planet,
a landfill, the very symbol of excess, waste,
and environmental harm? Had I become anesthetized
as waste management went from a cause to a way of life?
I hadn't created the system and was doing my best to keep
it clean, but somehow found myself the overseer of excess
and toxicity. Was I paranoid? How much of Lamb's theater
was about me, a way to stop the stories, to lay blame
and exact punishment for whatever behavior
he didn't like in his son? As clapping faded,
a smiling Lamb took his seat to a renewed
outburst of applause from his partisans.

"We're lucky to have Mr. Dempster with us tonight,"
Beryl said as if she was drowning and I held the life ring.
How did I ever get on the Republican side when I'd fought
Nixon and Reagan and never cast a GOP presidential ballot?
But Beryl was an old line party member with a heritage dating
back to her great grandfather, a Teddy Roosevelt Republican
who deburred buttons at Belcher and became state
representative in an age when it was the party
of progressivism in child labor, natural resources,

and standing up for the little guy. "As landfill super,"
Beryl was saying, "he may have some comments to enlighten
us." The room was silent as I rose to many icy stares.
I heard the Westmorland Press reporter tapping his laptop.

"At the outset, let me assure everyone that we follow all state
regulations to the letter," I began, as if compliance
with government requirements could inspire anyone's
confidence. "Contrary to what you've heard,
this is not a dump, it's a sanitary landfill with strict
requirements to place soil on the waste daily, erosion
measures, monitoring wells, vector and litter control,
and suppression of fugitive dust. To maximize
capacity and keep costs down we even compact individual
loads. Calculation of the slope shows that at current rates
the site will be full in five years. It will be capped
with an artificial membrane and clay, there will be methane
recovery and continued leachate monitoring. Contaminants
in the river are currently all within standards.
There's no huge plume threatening public health."
A disagreeable rumble in the crowd sounded like distant
thunder. "The landfill has been providing cost effective waste
disposal for decades, a necessity in any community.
Years ago, I would have echoed Mr. Lamb's concerns,
but scientific management has changed the calculus.
Our landfill is a community asset and an epic in the lives
of families who have used it for decades,
for whom garbage is not out-of-sight-out-of-mind,
but a part of seasonal and generational cycles
where we can show our kids the benefit of recycling
and the consequences of wasteful use of resources.
It is a living lesson for residents with value
beyond its mere function." I concluded to a soft, quickly
faltering clapping, caught a tepid smile from Beryl, and sat
down. I felt outside myself, as if watching my performance
with the rest of the audience. How far had I come to sound
like such a word-smoothing bureaucrat?

Popping up like a figure in the Whac-A-Mole carnival game,
Lamb didn't wait to be recognized. "With all due respect,
Mr. Dempster, this is not some sacred Indian burial mound."
Twitters of laughter echoed in the room.
"And as far as an example for kids, it's garbage,
garbage, garbage, and most of us don't want our kids playing
with trash. I'm not sure what state rules you follow,
but as far as I know state regulations forbid
scavenging. I don't know about others gathered here tonight,
but my son came home with this last week after handing
out my leaflets at the dump." Lamb almost shouted
as he held up a large, antiquated ceramic electric insulator
that must have tipped at fifteen pounds. It was a foot tall,
a glossy sepia-brown spiral. It's not the first time
it's happened and my son is not the only one.
You may have your reasons and excuses Mr. Dempster,
but the rules are the rules, and if we're not following
this one folks, we may well ask what else is awry.
This monstrosity of a mountain is a blister on our town
we need to treat before it bursts!"
he concluded, rhythmically pounding fist into palm.

INSULATOR DAZE

The next week disappeared in a daze,
    the selectmen's meeting replaying in my mind like a bad
    movie trailer or a traumatic accident regularly
revisited in slow motion. I slept with restless dreams
of the dump poisoning household wells that didn't exist,
of exploding methane gas spraying the town with trash
I had to pick up with a shovel and sharp stick.
What would I do without the dump, its daily routines
and familiar faces that were a community
as much as the regulars at the Third Base, Hawks Nest Pub,
or on the twilight league baseball team when Dad
started at shortstop for Belcher Button? It wasn't just a job,
but my home, my garden and sugar-woods.
In command of something important and essential,
I simultaneously reveled in being different, beyond the norm.
Where else could I be an outsider who was also an insider?
Hadn't I been doing good by the planet in promoting
recycling and following rules on hazmat and electronics?

Was the whole fiasco my own fault?
Buffaloed by the crowd, maybe I didn't make my case.
And that insulator. Justin didn't just pick it up wandering
the fill as Lamb intimated. Months ago, I'd gotten
off the dozer to grab it. That clunky thing stood forgotten

in front of the airstream the better part of a year before
catching the kid's eye. Besides, back in the day boys
like me snatched small treasures from the dump all the time—
light fixtures, pieces of wire or pipe, wheels
from worn out lawn mowers, and chunks of lumber.
It wasn't like I let pickers on the pile
scrounge for rags and scrap metal for sale.

I went through the motions, the routines,
but felt as if I'd never awakened, just stuck in a dream state,
everything hazy like those thick milky fogs of chilly
sublimating snow when sap runs slow and cold gets inside
the bones. My own voice seemed an echo, questions
and comments of others barely audible, only every second
and third word understood even from the loud talking Josh
Root, his unruly dark hair defying sixty plus years.
"How's the future park ranger," he quipped, tossing his *Time*
bundled skin mags into recycling. "You done a good job,
so don't take it personally. Had to end sometime. You got
time on your hands afterward, you mosey over to my place
and I'll keep you busy digging spuds come September.
I'm growin' Katahdins and Kennebecs this year, a few rows
of Yukon Gold." He grinned like a Halloween pumpkin
and slapped me on the back as he slid into his pickup.

Everyone had an opinion, and some, like Jack Ellyat, a geezer
of a truck driver who plowed for the town on contract
when a big one hit and whose family had been in town,
he like to say, "since Christ was a corporal,"
worried about the cost of throwing out his trash
and thought the notion of a park nutty.
"Sos the town gonna get into the garbage collecting business
now? And what genius calculated the cost of that?
If my ancestors knew it was going to come
to this, they would have stayed in England
and I'd be singing "God Save the Queen."
Ellyat's visits to the dump were never short if he caught
my ear. Always with a story, it might be about a missing

ancient merestone on his property, the Indian artifacts
his great grandfather found plowing, or the battles
his ancestors fought in the Revolution or Civil War.
"We still own a few hundred acres in the town's
north quarter and my taxes are through the goddamn roof
already. Imagine the seniors on fixed incomes. Got to agree
with you, the dump is cheap and well run. And jeez,
who the hell is gonna use that gazebo for weddings. I bet
people will just be falling over each other to tie the knot atop
a big crap pile." Laughing heartily at his own joke,
he looked up and saw something in my face.
"No offense," he added.
"None taken. It is what it is. Yup, a big crap pile."

Most folks took Root's view, that closing the dump
was inevitable and improved with a park. Some were wistful
and nostalgic, a few elders downright funereal over an ancient
community institution winding up. Here they regularly
recycled years of memories they'd be forced to toss
with the last of their trash as the gate locked for the last time.
Maybe gazebo weddings were a little over the top,
but young parents and folks with grandkids liked sports fields,
and a view of the valley you could climb to by car
appealed to seniors. I hadn't counted on so many dog owners
wanting a place for Rover, Fluffy, or Spotty to run
like Rin Tin Tin. If nothing else, Lamb knew to push buttons
that made things happen. Dumps were bad and parks
were good. Wasn't that our mantra at teach-ins and rallies
on that first Earth Day when I watched Senator Nelson
on a nineteen-inch rabbit-eared black-and-white from a couch
in the student union? Was I now just reaping what I'd sown?
Was this yet another step in getting back to the garden?
Had I gotten so turned around and lackadaisical
that I'd not only forgotten where I was going,
but where I'd come from? "Careful of that Lamb, fella,"
Jack Ellyat advised me in his old timey New England twang,
his A's flatter than a tin can come out of the compactor,
"that small-time nail banger ain't no Lamb. More like a wolf.

Truth be known, he's really a skunk. Son, you get into a fight
with him it don't matter whether you win or lose
'cause you're goin' to smell the same."

Sure it had to end sometime, but I never believed
it. We'd already passed two closure estimates because I ran
a good fill, compacted well and covered with minimal
material. With more going to recycling and the economy
slowed, we had less trash for the mound. Reviewing
the geometry a year ago, I contemplated a lateral extension
and kept meaning to ask Beryl if I could enter the bureaucratic
thicket. I guess I imagined keeping it going as far
as I could see, thought I had the know-how to have the fill
open forever. Had I fooled myself with the same old
optimism that strangled my high school and college years?

TIME TO RETURN

Late afternoon two days past the selectmen's meeting I sat in the Airstream sipping coffee, feeling as isolated as if berthed on the space station. Startled by a knock, I spilled a few drops in my lap. Visitors were rare since patrons liked me inside where I couldn't check for expired stickers or scrutinize their load and reject grass clippings in the leaf compost or collect the bulky waste charge. When someone came to the door it was usually for brush chipping, but rarely outside spring and fall. Figuring it was Beryl at last come to chat about her crash and burn board meeting, I responded to the second set of raps at the top of my voice. "If you don't like how that plastic babe's decked out, dress her up in your own lacy lingerie." I imagined her in tight jeans, bright lipstick and sensible heels. Expecting a smart aleck retort, I heard nothing. "Come on Beryl, you're a politician. I know you can cough up something snappy." After another long pause, I heard an unexpected voice.
"Mr. D., it's us," Justin said tentatively.
"Come in," I said, with a deep deflating sigh.

The door opened slowly and the boys shuffled in, unusually quiet and drained of puppy excitement. Justin grasped a large canvass tote bag. "We heard

you had a tough time at town hall," Justin said. "And even
though closing the landfill is good for the planet,"
Ralph continued, "we know you're a good steward."
Ralph forced a smile, took off his glasses and wiped
them on his tee shirt. "Yeah, no matter what, we're your
friends," Billy and Ronny said almost simultaneously.
Justin took a couple steps forward, opened the bag and pulled
out the big insulator. Out of context it looked like a piece
of modern art or a Japanese garden sculpture.
"I don't know how my dad got this. I kept it on the d.l.
but he spotted it in my room. You should take it back."
I shook my head. "It's okay," I said almost in a whisper.
"It doesn't matter."
Justin looked like he had a stomachache.
"Honest, I didn't tell anyone."
Nervous laughter escaped my lips. "I believe you."

"Tell us a funny story from your trip," Ronny proposed.
"A funny story?" They all nodded.
"Yeah," Ralph said, "it doesn't have to be a laugher,
just something a little weird, something real sweet
to shake the blues." I hesitated, leaning back
in my office chair to a bird-like squeak.
"Come on," Ronny pleaded in a good-buddy barroom way.
"Yeah," they chorused, "a funny story." The last thing I felt
was funny, and a change of subject was on my tongue
when a long locked-away memory seized me.

Twilight was fading just west of Grainfield, Kansas
when a bright green Chevy Impala pulled over ahead of me,
its headlights blazing into nothingness. The rear
was jacked up revealing twin chrome tailpipes that shone
in red sparkles reflected off the tail lights, the back window
detailed in a huge lopsided bowtie—the Chevy trademark—
with a stuffed dog peering through the middle, its eyes
lighting up when the brakes were pressed.
The car rumbled loudly, a growling animal.

Expecting a big, muscular guy with blue bicep tattoos,
I found a driver who was thin and soft-spoken with a twangy
down-home accent. Maybe a few years older than me, thick
tortoiseshell glasses framed a gentle farm-boy face.
We exchanged the usual greetings like grab-bag gifts.
He was on a mission about which, I guess, he had a hard time
telling his friends, so the sympathetic ear of a stranger,
especially a ghost of the road whom he'd never
see again, was just what he needed. We fell into fast
and easy intimacy as he spilled his story.

Jeremiah was a churchy person, fully-dunked-river-baptized
and in the choir doing his best to follow the footsteps of Jesus,
but now headed to settle a lawsuit in Ohio, where his sister
lived with her husband. Two years earlier when visiting
the newlyweds, they walked through a stubble-cut corn field,
not doing any harm or up to mischief, he took pains
to let me know. Out of a tumbledown shed in a copse of trees
at the edge of a windbreak came a farmer with a bulbous
nose below a feedcap brim aiming a side-by-side
and firing a load of rock salt. "Stung the three of us like a
hive of bees," he said, swallowing hard before
finishing his sentence, "and a big chunk caught my groin,
sent me to the hospital and cost me a testicle."

"Hit him in the Balls!" Justin exclaimed. "Talk about one
hung low," Ronny cackled, igniting peals of laughter.
"Real cool story, but you can't say that dude
was completely *nuts*," Ralph cracked, gasping for air.
I framed my hands in a time out T. "Guys," I said loudly to
get their attention, "that's not the funny part."
It took a moment for them to calm down
and they couldn't look at each other without a contagion
of giggles. "It was sad. He was so embarrassed,
and now had to go back to meet with lawyers
and try to settle things. Really guys."

*Hunched over the wheel he grasped with both hands,
Jeremiah drove the powerful machine slowly,
painfully so, as if he were expert with reigns holding back
an unruly draft horse. It might as well have been a VW bug
for all the gas he gave it. Keeping it steady
while losing me in legal and medical details, the engine
vibrated gently, cool, moist air pouring in with chatter
from the open window and drying my summer-night-sweat-
soaked shirt. Not knowing what to say, I punctuated
the story with sympathetic murmurs and sighs,
and an occasional question showing I was tuned in.
After about an hour he wound down, tension
leaking out as he leaned back in the seat
and seemed somewhat at ease, a single hand
on the wheel. I relaxed and nodded off.*

*Tires screeched and I felt myself falling forward.
Snapping up like a jack-in-the-box, I grabbed the dash
as we came out of the skid, Jeremiah bringing us to a stop
with the skill of an airline pilot on a difficult landing.
"What's wrong?" I asked frantically, half still in dreamland.
Blue and red police car lights flashing into the night
alternately blinded us with light and dark. "Holy Cow!
Look at them Chickens!" Jeremiah screeched with more
energy than I imagined it possible for him to muster.
Squinting into the revolving colored lights, I couldn't make
out a thing. Then I heard clucking and screeching
as several chickens dashed in front of our headlights
and disappeared into darkness. "Sounds like a passel
of coons let loose in a barnyard!" Jeremiah said.*

*Clacking, clicking, and cackling noises filled the night
as feathered, claw-footed, fleshy faced, head bobbing
chickens darted around the Chevy. Jeremiah hopped
from the car as a man in overalls charged out of the median
with a bird under each arm. "Darn deer run
out into the road. I stopped short and a couple dozen cages
fell outta the truck and broke," he said breathlessly, barely*

*able to speak as the chickens squirmed and pecked
to free themselves. I imagined a queer, three headed
creature, part man part bird. Still dazed,
I got out of the car as a hen ran between them, followed
closely by a state trooper, Smokey Bear hat
and all, as determined as a starved wild man. The driver
hurried back to his truck with his captives and Jeremiah
turned to me. "We got to help these people."*

*About to voice my doubts, Jeremiah darted off after a big
white bird leaving me wondering what to do. I'd never been
closer to a live chicken than a petting zoo.
Didn't they have diseases? And their beaks looked sharp.
Why was he so psyched to find these creatures
when he didn't even know the owner? They could belong
to some giant factory farm on their way to the slaughterhouse.
I imagined Sandoz screaming to free the chickens
like they were Black Panthers or something. But I joined
the pursuit, crawling under cars, dodging
between them, sprinting through tall grass and around
bushes. A dozen people chased strutting, half flying, bobble-
headed chickens in headlights and flashing colors,
running down the concrete interstate
and into the swales and brush alongside it.*

*"I was a pretty good tackle in high school,"
a hulking truck driver shouted to no one in particular
as he lay on his belly after lunging for a bird that he now held
clasped between palms. And it was like football, the chickens
expert in broken-field running and clearly favorites.
We were Keystone Cops, charging with that sped-up
old timey mechanical animation
through the splotchy, unevenly illuminated dark.*

*I got close to my quarry but once, as a coppery colored bird
pecked in grass at the edge of the breakdown lane.
Figuring it didn't see me, I snuck up on toe tips like a kid
playing tag, got within a yard, and as the bird bent its neck*

*for something in the dirt, I leaped through the air
and wrapped my arms around it snare-like.
Holding it momentarily fast, it let out such screeching
that I shrank back. It darted beneath a car and I was left
on my belly with bruised elbows and a few feathers in hand.*

*More cars stopped and soon we were twenty people running
up and down the road screaming and calling after chickens.
A fat guy got wedged under a pickup, the chicken pecking
at him just out of reach. Two men ran into each other,
one almost knocked unconscious. A cop, chicken in hand,
returned with the front of his uniform mud-blackened
from a fall into a drainage ditch. We played a far out,
poultry-roller-derby on an endless concrete track.*

*It wasn't a gut buster, but the boys were all smiles,
their minds spinning with bizarre images.
"Did they get all the chickens," Ralph wanted to know?
"As many as we could catch."
"I'll bet you dudes looked like poultry in motion," squeaky
voiced Ronny said, bombastically emphasizing his clever play
on words to universal groans. Justin took off his Red Sox
cap and gave Ronny a friendly smacking.
"I still think getting your balls shot off is funnier,"
he said to twittering giggles. "It would have been way-cool
if Sandoz was there leading the chicken liberation
front," he added, putting his cap back on.
"So what's the funniest Sandoz story," Billy challenged.
"There must have been some loony, maniac scenes."*

*We'd left Drop City just the day before and cruising
the steep Colorado mountains Sandoz took the car out of gear
as we coasted down hill, banking turns as if we were racing.
"Sangre de Cristo Creek" a sign announced as we crossed
a tiny twist of water and then ran headlong
through massive rocks. Pavement mimicked
the stream's crooks and bends, using the path carved
by water because engineers could do no better. Down
we went, the canyon widening until opening onto a grassy*

*plain with distant mountains. The road was lined with utility
poles and fence posts, and trees huddled beside modest
houses. Between doses of landscape my eyes darted
around the car, and I asked about a tiny red light blinking
erratically on the dash. "Oil," he said laconically,
and I suggested we stop to check the dipstick.
Tapping his fingers on the wheel and grinning,
he shook his head and told me to forget it. "But if we're low,
the engine could seize in the middle of nowhere,
I said. "Knock off the nervous grandma routine,
nowhere man sitting in your nowhere land.
Most of the time those lights don't mean a thing."
I bit my lip. "Most of the time?"*

*Sandoz was deep in one of his fugues
and talking with him was like awakening
someone from a dream, so I stared out the window.
Occasionally I'd glance at the dash where the light still
blinked. The dull red flash might as well have been a crying
baby and as hard as I tried I couldn't get my mind
off it. How could he be sure we didn't need oil?
What if the Chevy died out here miles from any help?
I waited a long several minutes.
"Sandoz," I said, "the light's still blinking."
"Yeah, so."
"Aren't you anxious we could be low on oil?"
"I told you, it's probably a screwy short."
"But this is the first time in a thousand miles
it's been on. Maybe it means something."
"Just forget it."
He was beginning to lose patience, but I continued
like a kid with unquenchable questions. "Yeah, but . . . ."*

*"Okay. If the light bothers you, I'll do something about
it and make you happy," he said sternly.
"We can stop in Alamosa for oil," I suggested.
"I told you we don't need oil. I'm going to fix the light.
Check the glove box for any tools." I pressed the button
and a bunch of crumpled papers, a dime bag of grass and a*

couple overripe, gooey soft apples tumbled to the floor.
"Only a tire pressure gauge and a screwdriver," I reported.

Sandoz seemed to increase his concentration on the road, press a little harder on the gas. Thinking he hadn't heard me, I was about to repeat the tool inventory when he asked for an apple. Reaching down, I grabbed one. "It's kinda gross from the floor," I said. "Will you just hand me the freakin' apple, and the screwdriver, too."
"Screwdriver?"
"Stop Bogarting and hand them over already. You want the light fixed so I'm fixing the freaking light." Sandoz bit into the puffy fruit, took a few bites and then held it clenched in his teeth as juice ran down his chin and dripped onto his shirt. In his left hand he held the steering wheel, and with the screwdriver clutched firmly in his right fist began jabbing the dashboard. Letting out an apple muffled, but still loud demented laugh that made me jump, he stabbed the dashboard repeatedly until the light was not only out, but nowhere to be seen, only a hole where it had blinked so nervously. He handed back the screwdriver, took the apple out of his mouth and began taking bites again. "You satisfied now?" he asked. I just nodded, tossing the tool back into the glove box. "You can have the other apple, if you want," he said.

"What a wild and crazy dude," Ronny said, whistling through the gap in his teeth. "I'd be afraid of shorting out the electrical system, especially on that funky old jalopy."
"Maybe," Justin said, "but you gotta admire a guy with a sixth sense about cars, 'cause the light may be on, but he obviously knows what his engine needs, probably just by listening."
I shook my head. "He had no idea. Next time we gassed up the attendant checked the oil after washing the windows and turns out we were down two quarts."
Ronny whistled again. "Wow! Someone washed your windows!"

GHOSTS PAST

Like a ride into the old neighborhood left years
in the rearview, the memories come flooding back in bits
and pieces, incoherent fragments as vivid
and disconnected as dreams. I'm frightened
even as I welcome them, like the relief
that must come to drowning
men when they give up the panicked struggle and surrender
to a deep breath of water filling air-starved lungs.

U.S. PLANS TO ORDER AIR BAGS IN AUTOS

elected Hayakawa permanent president of S.F. State—
a move that almost guarantees more strife

PRESIDENT EASES SCHOOL DEADLINE
ON DESEGREGATION

NADER SAYS NEW STUDIES SHOW
TAINTED SEAFOOD

PENTAGON DENIED FUNDS
TO DEVELOP CHEMICAL ARMS

ME AND MY WINSTON'S ... WE GOT
A REAL GOOD THING

"The policeman isn't there to create disorder, the policeman is there to preserve disorder," said Mayor Daley

DUMP DUSTUP

Hot, garbage stewing in the heat, smells wafting
in waves on a droughty breeze blowing dust from the top
of the fill, my dozer idled ready to spread the daily cover.
With a dog's olfactory acuity I recognized the overripe odor
of rotting vegetables (probably left too long in the fridge),
the putrid smell of table scraps, sickly sweet scent
of greasy delights like leftover fries from the Third Base
and other restaurants, the honeyed musty smell of sun-baked
plastics from toys, kitchen gadgets, or empty containers,
and earth-spicy leaves toasting on the compost pile.
Shadows of wavering heat rose ghost-like from the pavement,
and my tee shirt clung to my back with sweat and dirt.
Streams of perspiration followed age creases
in my face below the slight shade of a Red Sox cap.

Just a few minutes till closing and I was eager to be done,
feeling the weight of a long sunny day,
needing to water my wilting tomatoes and eggplants,
debating whether I had energy enough to thin carrots again,
or hoe the heat thriving weeds from the bean hills.
Just as I reached the chain link gate two pickups
pulled in: Zeke Reid, a tin knocker from just down the road,
in his big battered F-250 with an exhaust like a continuous
Bronx cheer, and Mickey Lamb behind the wheel

of his metallic blue Silverado with its gothic red lettered door
advertising ML Construction in a triangular logo.
Reid had a big rehab job on Winsted's Main Street, snaking
ductwork through a century-old brick storefront
with apartments above. He'd dump empty adhesive tubes,
strips of plastic that wrapped galvanized sheet metal,
corrugated boxes and little pieces of sheetrock
and wood. Lamb was a little more unpredictable,
but it was usually small scale demolition, scrap wood, joint
compound buckets and the like. Since one of his dozer
operators got pinched burying demo, he'd been bringing a lot
more of it. Scuttlebutt says it was a business SOP,
but the equipment operator took the hit and Lamb came off
smelling like a rose, a guy who strictly disciplined
his sometimes misguided workers to follow the rules.

As Lamb drove in, the daisy-faced clock I'd salvaged
from the swap shack and hung on a pole hit three and I swung
the gate closed, waiting until the trucks were emptied
and gone before clasping the lock. Reid was quick, stopped
where I thought he would, tossing construction debris
into the rolloff and then a couple black bags of household
to the compactor. He rumbled out with a wave as I shut
the gate behind him. Lamb moved slowly, seeming to place
each piece of scrap wood and shard of sheetrock
in the big steel container one at a time as if he were offloading
glassware. By the time he reached the recycling with bags
of paper, I itched with impatience, overheated in the blazing
sun. He appeared to spill flyers, receipts and photocopied
sheets on the ground, some skipping away along the bumpy
macadam and sailing on the breeze toward the fence.
What the hell, I thought, and walked over.

Lamb was rightly throwing stuff into the new single stream
recycling, but seemed purposefully sloppy
so that about half the paper, plastic and glass fell
to the ground. "Please try to get it in the bin," I said politely,
as I walked toward him. Lamb seemed not to hear,

though I was plenty loud. He'd eyed me walking across
the yard, but now that my shadow lay across the material
he was spilling, he acted like I wasn't there. I repeated
my plea in as gentle a manner as I could muster.
He turned toward me, his face again fist-like, and dropped
a packet of papers at my feet. "I pay my taxes.
Isn't that what you're hired for—to clean up this shit?"
Anger rose like an irresistible belch, but I ignored
the challenge. "It's hot and I still have to cover the trash
and backblade it smooth before clocking out. The town's
in a budget bind and Beryl says no overtime
so I best not be picking up litter."
"You tell Beryl to stuff it up her raggy old twat.
I'm gonna whip her fat ass in the election
and you won't have to worry about her."
"Be like everyone else," I said sharply, "and please pick up."

"I told you to stop filling my kid's mind with crap.
When his mother, who'd just as soon see me on hell's
rotisserie, calls to say she's worried, I pay attention.
I didn't divorce that whoring bitch for nothing and we hardly
talk, so when she's on the phone I know something's really
wrong." Lamb moved a step closer, emptying a full
bag of papers at my feet. I felt the full bulk of his body
leaning over me like a tree about to fall. "I'm not interested
in what's going on between you and your ex."
"And you don't have to be. It's about my kid."
"I told you, he and his buddies come on their own.
So what if they help with sugaring and gardening
and I tell them some stories they want to hear."
"You're polluting their minds as much as the groundwater.
You're a Pied Piper of poison, dumping on impressionable
kids with your hopeless failed hippie shit no one wants
any more than stinking trash."
"You'll be happy to know they haven't been listening
to many stories recently. They're handing out your leaflets."
"Your damn right! And when I empty Proulx's desk drawers
in the dumpster it'll be one of the last loads

you'll see because this wart on the town
is going to close and you'll be out on your ass."
"Just calm down and clean up your mess.
This isn't about Justin or the election."
"When my kid starts painting a hippie bus
in his mother's driveway where he thinks
I won't find out about it, I know who's to blame."
"That's between you and Justin. Right now
we're talking about a law that says waste
has to be disposed of in proper containers."

Lamb rose to full height like a cornered bear
and I could see his muscles tightening, nostrils flaring.
I wanted to return my own barrage of verbal bombs,
but he was dangerous and I needed to measure words
carefully. "Soon I'll be saying what the law
is, and this place will be locked tighter than a cat's ass.
You'll be flipping burgers for your buddy
Nicki Kakrides and living in a third story walk-up
with a leaking roof in Winsted."
Reaching into the pickup bed, he grabbed a plastic barrel
of kitchen garbage which must have been sitting
in the heat a few days and emptied it in front of me.
"Damn-it Lamb, pick up your own fucking trash
and get out of here! I've got work to do."

With a stiff shove, I tripped over the trash and sunglasses
and cap went flying as I fell backwards,
landing on my side, right shoulder taking the brunt.
"If you think it's so important, pick up the crap yourself,"
he said, sweet with sarcasm.
My nostrils filled with the smell of rotting garbage,
and flies buzzed around me like stars circling a cartoon
character that's been whacked aside the head.
"I'll let myself out, thank you very much,"
Lamb said, grinning with hands on hips. The truck door
slammed, he gunned the motor and peeled
out in a squeal of exhaust and tire-spun gravel.

THE FIND

Left in a daze, insects buzzing around me, elbow
throbbing and sun baking, rage came like waves of heat,
embarrassment like sunburn, a penumbra
of pain. In today's version of a Wild West gunslinger,
I thought to draw my cell phone and fire a 911 cop call.
But except for a scraped elbow, I was alright. Besides,
regardless of being right and hungering to beat this skunk,
Jack Ellyat was spot-on and going toe-to-toe with Lamb
would only make me smell worse. It would be my word
against his in a town where he always got a pass.
Sure he had a temper and said things he shouldn't, was a bully
some barflies nicknamed "The Rooster,"
but he was known as a guy who got things done
and would give you the shirt-off-his-back in a pinch.
Easy to rile and impulsive, Mickey Lamb was still a pillar
of the community. Considered a good guy, he donated
equipment and labor to build a new soccer
field and put a roof on town hall at cost. His picture
made the local weekly when he took the winning girls
basketball team out to the Third Base for breakfast
on a Saturday morning and threw a pizza party
for Little Leaguers who missed
a regional championship by an unearned run.

Even if I didn't mind the skunk smell,
our versions of events would cross like swords,
a he-said, she-said that would go nowhere.
He'd concoct some cock-and-bull that fingered me as angry
and eager for revenge because he'd proposed to steal
my livelihood and life. Loss of my job and home
would be clear motivation to any tongue-wagging gossip.
Reporting him and pressing charges was a loser.
I had to find another way. Maybe I could tell those kids
some wild stories, encourage them in their merry
Kesey bus and watch Lamb explode.

Dusting myself off, I flexed a sore elbow like a hit-by-a-pitch
batter shaking off pain. Back in the airstream,
some water, antibacterial cream and a bandage soothed
my worry, if not the ache. I returned to Lamb's mess, picked
up my hat and glasses and, putting on gloves, began sorting
the stuff—garbage to the maw of the compactor,
recycling into the single stream rolloff. It looked like Lamb
had been living pretty high with lobster shards and maggoty
rib roast bones and lots of oyster shells, but he let his fruits
and vegetables go bad. He was drinking Samuel Smith's
Oatmeal Stout, Johnny Walker Blue and can after can of Coke
on which he didn't collect deposits. He must have cleaned
out his files because there was a flurry of old lumberyard
invoices for shingles and spruce studs, plywood,
hinges and other hardware along with plumbing supplies
like copper pipe, faucets and toilets.
There were bid documents for roofs, roads, driveways
and pouring foundations; magazines like Popular Mechanics
and National Geographic; installation instructions
for cabinets and furnaces; plans sketched on paper scraps.

Anyone working in an office knows the danger of paper clips,
how one document accidentally attaches to another
and disappears into the wrong file, gets lost in a stack
or is sent to a party whose eyes were not meant
to see it. They're ingenious, convenient, but potentially

self-defeating devices for unsuspecting secretaries, students
or businessmen. Among the stapled and bound papers,
was a clip sharp and splayed at an odd angle, bent
and pointing like a half open jackknife. It sliced my finger,
blood spilling over attached old magazine articles
about pouring concrete in wet weather
and repairing backhoe hydraulics. But for the cut,
I'd have tossed all into the never-land
of the recycling bin without looking, including my ticket
for settling with Lamb. Caught among
the instructional articles were slightly faded and now blood
spotted emails about five years old between Lamb
and his foreman, clearly showing the contactor had ordered
a wetland filled with demolition waste from another job,
an act blamed on the dozer driver and for which, the email
indicated, the operator got an extra payday for silence,
far less than the money saved by illegal burial.

I felt light as I climbed to the idling Deere,
as if the day's dulling heat and humidity had vaporized
in a cool autumn breeze. Momentarily intoxicated
with a vengeful power, the throb of pain faded
and almost disappeared. Over the years I'd read a lot about
October surprises on election eves and now I had a weapon
to shoot down the high flying contractor
become pseudo environmentalist who wanted to close
my landfill and alter the arc of my life. I carried
the documents up hill to the dozer, each step deliberate,
measured, as if I held a winning lottery ticket
I'd hoped for over decades.   By the time
I reached the rumbling diesel, the paper felt as weighty
as Moses' stone tablets of shalt nots.
I looked out at the rolling landscape filled with trees
and followed the winding gray ribbon of river to clearings
dotted with houses and then to the white steepled churches
needling the sky and the brownstone
clock tower marking the center of town, places
where judgments would be made from the pulpit and ballot

box. In a euphoria of triumph that proved as brief
and illusory as a drunk or pot-smoked high,
I folded the documents and placed
them in the chest pocket closest to my heart.

MY PRECIOUS

In zombie dreams spawned by my game changing power,
I schemed and re-schemed, one scenario after another playing
quick movies in my mind like the rapid fire, action-cluttered
film trailers booming in theaters before the feature.
Would I send the orphaned email anonymously to the paper,
drop it like a foundling on a desk at town hall, post
it on Facebook, or call a big press conference on the landfill's
ragged slopes? I thought of timing, and calendar pages
danced before my eyes, falling away like in some
1940s black-and-white drama. Should I mount
an election eve surprise or announce it well in advance,
slowly letting momentum leak from Lamb's campaign like air
from a tire? I imagined angry heckling at a town meeting,
spaghetti dinner fundraisers filled with empty tables,
and back-peddling and winy explanations that would raise
the ire of voters and be lampooned by commentators,
columnists and the self appointed pundits at the Third Base,
the Hawk's Nest and the firehouse.

Back in the Airstream, I broke from a trance and cold sweat,
at last in the present again, only vaguely recalling climbing
aboard the dozer, covering, compacting and back-blading
the day's trash with soil and returning to the office.
It seemed something remembered from long ago.

I took the paper from my pocket and slowly unfolded
it, smoothed it on the old door that was my desk,
bending the folds back, rubbing the dog-eared
edges, flattening, straightening, wiping a few soiled
spots mostly clean. It was suddenly a talisman, a holy relic,
a symbol of power like a judge's gavel or monarch's mace.
I read it and reread it, a holy document more than the sum
of its words. I slipped it into a plastic sleeve and manila
folder and slid it far back into the only file drawer that locked.
Unable to work and the hour already late, I left the office
and turned the key in the door until I heard it click,
something I never did.

Over the next few nights, Lamb's accidental confession
infiltrated my sleep in bright colors and voices
that startled me in mid snore. The nightmare email
transfigured sometimes into a huge light-refracting diamond,
a gold coin, sun-glinting knife, shiny red Corvette,
or 30 round AR-15. It was money, it was power, it was lethal
authority and I cherished it even as it frightened
me with cold sweats and loathing. How to best use this crime
scene fingerprint, this smoking gun? It haunted
me, and where at first I was high on these mental movies,
reveled in carefully polishing ideas to topple Lamb,
now they would not let me rest. I felt trapped
by my new found freedom to do something, bloated
with ache like too much of a favorite food.

Four days after the find, I was rearranging the swap shack,
tossing the plates and old books that after a month had worn
out their welcome, the chipped glassware and knick-knacks
that no one wanted, the bicycle wheel missing all but six
spokes, a broken toilet seat, and an aquarium
with cracked glass. I rearranged the logo mugs
from sports teams and bank promotions, rusted garden tools,
boxes of infant toys, rubber banded bundles of pencils
and pens, and copper-bottomed and stainless pots and pans.
Gathering a bunch of VHS videos, I rearranged them neatly

on a shelf. I rarely rented or went to the library,
instead borrowing flicks from those offered here for free.
Bummed at no new ones this time, I recalled the parody
slapstick of Mel Brooks' *Spaceballs*, the haunting mystery
of *Apocalypse Now*, and Robin Williams' manic performance
as the DJ in *Good Morning Vietnam* while carefully
reshelving them. Along with several Disney films,
including *The Little Mermaid* and *The Lion King*,
that must have been left by Francie Dodson
with whom I'd had had a long conversation about clearing
out her highschooler's room while I tended a clog
in the compactor, I found the *Lord of the Rings*. The trilogy
had fueled my college imagination in print and later my adult
longings on the screen with its grand sweeping
landscapes and world-in-the-balance drama.

Recalling that quirky cadre of characters from hobbits
to dwarves and elves, I fell into a daydream reverie
over Gandalf and Frodo, Bilbo Baggins, Tom Bombadil
on the Barrow Downs, and wraith-like Gollum with his horrid
gulping swallow and fetish for the gold ring of power,
his precious. The gleeful endorphins of imagination played
like soft shadows on the wall of the shack while I tidied
and acted as executioner for objects that would never
again see daylight or the clutch of human hands.

Almost done, I stopped cold. In a moment of lightening-like
free association, Lamb's email was suddenly joined
to Gollum's ring, both sources of power. Was I not coveting
this paper like the golden hoop the skeletal creature craved?
I had it tucked away in my cave-like Airstream, hidden
in the dark recesses of a cabinet where I thought no one could
find it. For days I'd obsessed, my thoughts hijacked.
Would I waste away to cadaverous monomania
like Tolkien's bug-eyed creation with his leer and lisp, eaten
away as if by some flesh devouring bacteria? Growing dizzy,
nausea overtook me like sudden onset flu.

TRANSFORMERS

Hurrying to the trailer, holding the urge to gag, I grabbed
the small key hidden under an old turtle shell
I'd found at the edge of the fill, turned it in the lock, opened
the drawer and pulled the folder. It seemed heavy, almost hot.
One foot on solid ground and another feeling as if I'd stepped
into an LSD flashback, the world seemed to teeter,
all at the edge of vision. Embarrassed by my fixation,
this obsession plotting Lamb's political demise
seemed the stuff of craziness. The notion that possession
could transform me, like the sniveling, paranoid
wraith of the ring, seemed equally fantastic, another crack
in reality. Gollum, so named for the repetitive sound
of his swallowed phlegm, was once, as Tolkien told, a playful,
if mischievous and misguided boy who killed his companion
under the spell of the shiny ring. Could my scheming
have the same power to transform?
I didn't want Lamb to turn me into something I wasn't,
something like him, as Jack Ellyat prophesized about skunks.

Maybe closing the fill wasn't so bad despite Lamb's turbid
motivations and self-serving back-alley dealing.
Was I selfish, shortsighted, too entangled in my own
dependency on the big trash pile? Parks "were" good,
and toxics, pollution, and conspicuous consumption festered

at dumps. Had I forgotten what grounded
me back in sixty-eight handing out leaflets for Gene?
Thoughts paced nervously back and forth in my brain.
Was Lamb beyond positive transformation? Maybe the issues
swirling around Justin were clouding not just his, but my own
judgment. The kid's campaigning might even heal
their relationship. It seemed to be working. Maybe I should
give Lamb a pass as I did for Sandoz
all those years ago. We all had a past, and some of us,
like Jack Ellyat, basked in family lore,
while others wanted to box it and deep six the package
in some fathomless sea. Had I lied to the kids, cheated
them of reality's complexity because I hadn't told them about
the hidden history held tight by that wild man of the road,
that Dean Moriarty and Neal Cassady wannabe.

Returning from Cody's hilltop birthday party
the night before we barreled out of Drop, I was mellowed
out, dry-throated and buzzed from an afternoon of endlessly
orbiting joints. My rubbery legs stumbled along the dark
rocky path, though a star pricked sky lit
the landscape like dusk. Quickening breezes blew away
the day's warmth and a chill crawled up my spine
so I made to Sandoz's car for my coat, an Ike jacket my father
had worn in the army. Bathing in the camaraderie of the day,
I was bursting with joy in a place I at last felt accepted
and valued. My mind played an endless loop of Dylan's
creaky voice and simple guitar chords. "Oh to dance beneath
the diamond sky with one hand waiving free,
silhouetted by the sea, circled by the circus . . . ."
I skipped and pivoted, became one with the evening.

The door handle was cold and with a screaking scrape
of metal on metal it opened. To my amazement the overhead
light clicked on with a weak, pale yellow glow, the color
of a flashlight at the end of its batteries. Not seeing
the jacket, I rummaged around in the jumble of bags, boxes
and pieces of rumpled clothing tossed into the seatless

*rear of the car until I found it under a nest of old newspapers.
Starting to shiver, I yanked the sleeve sending a couple empty
wine bottles and a large, battered White Owl cigar box flying.
The bottles rolled out the door with a clatter, and the box
opened, spilling its contents where the jacket had been.*

*I bent to pick up the box and froze. No stogies
littered the rusted Chevy floor. Instead,
there was a tarnished, monogrammed silver baby's spoon
and a bronzed bootie, a black and white photo of a duplex
house and a picture of a man who looked vaguely like Sandoz
wearing a World War II corporal's uniform.
A set of chevrons were stapled to the photo. There was a roll
of Indian head pennies and a soiled high school diploma
granted to a Richard Stevens from some Podunk Pennsylvania
town. I felt the heat of embarrassment and began replacing
everything as quickly and neatly as I could.
There was something wrong about touching these things,
and felt as if I'd accidentally walked in on someone
undressing, or had knocked over a towering pyramid
of supermarket cans. There were more photographs
and small items like a few marbles and a shriveled horse
chestnut. Every time I replaced one thing I discovered
another loose on the floor. There were yellowed news
clippings about a high school track
team with the name "Richard Stevens" underlined in red ink,
a gold chain with a cross attached, and an Eagle Scout
badge admonishing: "Always Be Prepared."*

*Things spilled from the box became surreal
and seemed to glow, absorbing and reflecting
the candle-yellow light overhead. For all Sandoz's evasive
disregard of the past, he actually held it close, relics
and talismans of a life submerged. As much as he might play
with my questions and respond in riddles, answers
were always with him, concretely available and tucked
away. How really free was he and of what?
Why did he need to be so mysterious?*

Could his craziness amount only to theater,
an invention of the road, an escape, a way to exalt
who he wanted to be over who he was?
I never called him on it, never hinted at what I'd found
and what I suspected. Was I afraid that he'd drop
me on some lonely stretch of road, or that I might be flashing
bourgeois bias and not seem hip? Maybe I needed to believe
in Sandoz as much as he needed to perform.
Though we emerged from the same middle class suburban
world, only he had the guts to step beyond.
Maybe I wanted to be Sandoz, but couldn't. In school
we learned that people taking the main chance
and remaking themselves was the hunger at the heart
of America. The self-made man wasn't just about money,
but moving on from one frontier to another, from job to job,
even name to name in a constant process of reinvention
as rich as the mechanical ingenuity that earned patents
and built a world of manufactured goods and military might.

Had I made a mistake giving Sandoz a pass?
Was his act fantasy or alternate reality?
Was Lamb's political theater so different from Sandoz's
performance? Maybe people should be able to live
out their thespian lives until they trip themselves up,
get tangled in their own stories.
Was I a cop arresting renewal, rebuilding, and rebirth
in an age where internet and social media tempted
with easy transformations? Was this now the frontier's edge?
Who was I to bludgeon Lamb with his past, prevent him
from doing environmental good despite polluted motives?

GHOSTS PRESENT

What is buried and seething sometimes wells
up at a holiday, a birthday, or a historic anniversary like Earth
Day, Medgar Evers murder, or the Kent State Massacre,
which no one seems to remember.
Past times no more disappear than Mount St. Helens
and sister volcanoes are dead of lava rage after quiescent
generations. What was left behind comes back like the reissue
of a book or old flick, or is stirred by tell-all memoirs,
a new Dylan album or the geriatric
Stones on one last tour. The power is deep, silent, explosive.

U.S. JUDGE DELAYS WIRETAP RULING
IN CHICAGO RIOTS

How many roads must a man walk

KENNEDY FACES CHARGE FOR LEAVING
CRASH SITE—CAREER IMPERILED

asked Joan Baez how it would feel to have her first
child with David in jail. "I'm having it by natural
childbirth so I hope in feels good"

HANOI AIDE CHARGES U.S. INVADES LAOS

Senator Eugene McCarthy said today he would not
seek reelection

EVERYBODY WHO'S BEEN TO THE MOON IS EATING STOUFFERS

sentenced Cassius Clay to five years in prison and a $10,000
fine on the charge of refusing induction

ELECTED, SELECTED

I couldn't contain it and didn't want to tell anyone,
but Lamb's email was too much to hold myself. I climbed
the brownstone steps of town hall, cupped with a century
of shoe-leather, and entered beneath the granite
arch into an echoing dark atrium where a heart-shaped
stairway led to the second floor. I passed the town clerk's
office, always alive with dog and fishing license gossip, taxes
paid and owed, real estate deals and the thump of big books
pulled from shelves of a steel-doored vault where the parceled
biography and bible of town-life lay for all to see.
I went up the stairs to echoing footsteps and the soft rising
sound of office chatter from doors ajar, not having taken
the elevator since childhood, an old Otis with a sliding mesh
grate. But today I wished I'd ridden the ancient
birdcage because the gentle bubble of sound seemed harsh,
loud even, as I carried my burden. It was early
and I saw no one, yet felt as if eyes were on me.
I was Frodo approaching Mount Doom in the heart
of Mordor, struggling with his will and the ring's
gathering weight though all I had was a manila envelope
and several sheets of printed paper. I felt as if I was carrying
two five gallon pails of sap after a full day
at the evaporator. All I'd done was pick
up a few sheets of paper among thousands trashed
each week. I had evidence of a crime, yet felt guilty.

I came to a dark wooden door framing a large sheet of frosted
glass through which I saw a shadow at a desk. After rapping
on the pane just above gold, black-edged lettering reading
"Beryl Proulx, First Selectman," her high pitched
canary-like voice welcomed me with a singsong.
Swinging the door, I was hit by the earthy musk
of her perfume and a big smile of surprise and welcome.
"Wow! To what do I owe the honor of this visit?
I'm at your place a couple months ago and now here you
are. I like symmetry, but people will talk like old times."
"You admired my digs so much, I thought you needed to
redecorate. I brought you a few gifts from the landfill—
a cracked garden gnome, a model airplane with one wing,
a poster from last year's firemen's jamboree,
and a few chipped commemorative plates from Niagara Falls
suitable for hanging on the wall," I said, looking around
an office with a couple old filing cabinets, three bentwood
chairs and walls covered with signed photos of politicians
and local celebrities, awards from the Rotary, League
of Women Voters, Chamber of Commerce,
and Regional Council of Governments as well as photos
of Little League teams, Scout troops and overseas exchange
students the town had sponsored. In a corner were a couple
shovels with blades spray-painted gold from some ground
breaking. "The gnomes and all that other stuff's
in that envelope?" she asked, and I realized
that momentarily I'd forgotten Lamb's email.

"The stuff is in the truck. There's so much,
I gotta go back for another load."
She shook her head and smiled. "Wait till
you see the mannequin I got for you. And this time
the bra fits, so you got nothing to complain about."
"A fitting bra? Not very realistic."
"You always seem to manage a good fit," I said, staring at the
soft, well defined curves of her striped blouse.
"How would you know? Back in the day your hand was
quicker than your eye. I can't believe you noticed."

"Beryl, it was a long time ago," I said, releasing a long, deep
breath. "And I did notice, at least once."
"Oh, when was that?"
"The time you fooled me with that front closure."
"Yes, a little paradise by the dashboard light, and then some,"
she said, leaning back in her chair and briefly glancing
at the ceiling with its water stained acoustical tile.
I completed the thought. "Yes. Doubly blessed.
Barely seventeen and barely dressed." A quick
smile stole over me and just as quickly evaporated.
After all these years I was still attracted
to her and she knew it. Sometimes I think she'd flip her hair
or smooth her skirt just to tease me. I never said anything,
because I didn't want her to stop. "I guess we could
have had something," I said, almost under my breath.
"Maybe. We were shipwrecked by wrestling personalities,
time away at college, religion, feuding parents, and maybe
the thought that we could both do better."
"Which neither of us ever did."
"So after all these years you at last bring me a love letter,"
she said with a laugh that took me back to high school.
It was the laugh that first drew my attention among
all the sweet-sixteen hard-bodies, expressing a kind of
insouciant delight that clutched my heart
and grabbed for my groin.
"Not exactly. But maybe it will help both of us."
I handed her the envelope. She opened it gingerly
and reached for glasses hanging on a chain around her neck.

Finished reading, she lay the papers on her desk,
pulled off the tortoise shell half-frames and paused
with one of the ear pieces to her lip.
"It's a smoking gun," I said.
"But the barrel's cold, the smoke long gone."
"Are you talking about Lamb bulldozing wetlands or our
relationship? We got him here in black and white. Rumors
have percolated for years and now there's proof.

You know as well as I do that this is just the tip
of the iceberg. If he gets prosecuted, they'll find more."
"Calm down, Caleb. Don't get your bowels
in an uproar. This isn't Watergate."
"So it's wetlandsgate. Same difference.
This is the way to beat him. We save the landfill
and you get reelected. It's a win, win."
"I wish it were so simple, but even if this winds
up in headlines I doubt it'll change the election.
Mickey will come up with some slantwise story, maybe even
say he's been framed. He'll no doubt use the word crucified.
Voters will see it as a ploy by two people feeding at the public
trough too long and wanting to save their cushy government
jobs and pad their pensions. Besides,
the statute of limitations has probably passed."

"So you're giving up? You're going to let
that bigmouth prick take over this town."
"He's not taking over. Trust me, after all these years I know
one thing for sure. Sitting in this chair doesn't make you
king, not even for a day. Everyone has an opinion, sometimes
multiple contradictory ones. To get anything done
you have to answer to the other selectmen and the board
of finance and do it all in a way that isn't going to alienate
most of the voters and the loudmouth letter-to-the-editor,
grandstanding-at-town-meeting types. And then, if a town
employee who is supposed to carry out a project
doesn't like something, try getting it done right and on time
without divine intervention. And worst of all is the trivial
bullshit that bogs you down. You know why I have to kick
you out in a few minutes? Because I have to listen
to a guy appeal his fine for not clearing snow off his sidewalk
last winter. After that, I have a meeting with Donald Hough,
a deacon at the Congregational Church when we were kids.
Remember how we'd sneak into his yard at night and skinny
dip in his pool. He wants the town to do something about
the squirrels that keep falling in and drowning."

"Old man Hough still swims?"
"No, but his grandchildren and great grandchildren do."

"You're just burnt out. Sad. I never
thought I'd see that. You're giving into the political bullshit."
"I've been in politics long enough to know how things work.
Folks are ready for change and Mickey has lots of friends.
With his equipment and know-how he's got a lot of chits.
And its good stuff like sports fields and repairs
on this crazy town hall roof at cost. Saved us a fortune."
"But he's a con man, a fraud."
"Folks know he plays a little fast and loose,
but they see him as a can-do guy, someone who cuts
through red tape and gets things done. He's given a lot
of people paychecks and has a boatload of favors to cash in."
"I can't believe you're giving up."
"Caleb, I'm still campaigning full bore, but I've been
knocking on doors, going to meetings every night,
and have my ear to the ground. I know what's going on."
"Why haven't I seen you at the dump passing out flyers?"
"I'll get there eventually, but it's not very effective. Most
people are annoyed. No one wants to linger at the landfill."
"Lamb has those kids there all the time."
"The kids are cute, and young and strong enough to help
people dump their trash." I stood up.
"Beryl, you're tossing away the key to winning."
"Don't go yet," she half pleaded. "Look, I know the score,
but I don't want to win with some Nixon-like dirty trick."
"He's a prick and guilty as sin! How can you let him get
away with this? My Dad worked construction,
and did it without hurting so much as a frog."

"Is that what's driving you Caleb, nostalgia for your Dad,
a lost childhood? So you of all people must understand that
for Mickey this campaign is as much about winning back
his son as running the town. He's going balls to the wall
and your not going to stop him. It's personal.

Besides, I want to see him twist in the wind as much
as you do. Trust me, when you sit in this chair
nothing is secret. The press and public sniff out every
stinking fact given enough time. Your sweetest
revenge, if that's what you want, would be to let him win."
"He's a fraud and a phony. It'd be so damn wrong."

"I'm just realistic. It's not that I don't get the injustice part.
And I know it's not only about your job,
but I also know about bad blood between you and Lamb.
Listen, from the day the town decides to close
the landfill it'll take at least two years. You know
as well as anyone that we've got a closure
plan to revise, and a search for disposal alternatives
that needs new specs and bidding. By that time
the dump would be shuttered anyway."
"I've got management techniques that'll make it last
longer and save tons of cash over any alternative."
"I'm sure, but the point is, there's an end in sight."
"I'm not sure I see the point."
Beryl leaned back in her chair and let out a sigh that emptied
her lungs and seemed to leave her tired, sunken.
"Caleb, you know how I feel about you even though things
didn't work for us all those years ago for reasons I barely
remember. Still, there's always been chemistry
between us and we've always done right by each other.
All my years in politics, I've championed your operation
because you're honest, economically shrewd, and turned a
blight into a model of earth stewardship and environmental
education. Don't get mad when I tell you something right
from the heart. I know that . . ."
The old fashioned black phone on her desk rang.
"Please have him wait," she said into the receiver.
"I'll be with him in a few minutes."
"Should I leave?"
"Please stay. There's something I need to say."

"This is your chance to break free. You fell into this dump
gig early and never launched, never got to explore a wider
world. Now's the time to do something you really want
to do. You've been hiding all these years, stifled by the job."
"How can you say that? Look at yourself.
What about those big political ideals? You wanted
to be the first female U.S. Senator from this state
and you spend your time in this tiny one stoplight town
and end up caving to a crooked contractor."
"Caleb, just listen to me for a moment."
"Okay, all ears."
"I didn't give up or settle for less. Sure, you can make
a difference in higher office, but it's a lot of political
pontificating and logrolling compromises and big money
fundraising on issues so large they have little affect
on everyday people. Early on I realized I could have more
impact close to the source and not only get government
working, but restore faith with transparency and availability,
keeping taxes reasonable and at the same time paving roads,
building a new senior center, funding the library
as the community's cultural heart, and ensuring the post office
didn't leave downtown. I've made a difference
in real lives that's not possible wrapped in the beltway."

"Beryl, listen to yourself. You sound like a stump speech.
How is it you get to lower your sights, but my work
somehow is a waste and I'm less than I should be?"
"Your words not mine. I didn't say that."
"How about promoting recycling and the Swap Shack,
being a pollution watchdog, extending the landfill's
life as a cost effective solution for thousands.
Doesn't that mean anything?"
"I told you, I admire that you've turned a sow's ear . . ."
She slapped her hand on the desk. "I just want you to see . . ."
"And I've touched a lot of people in town,
advocating for the environment, helping the elderly
with their trash. When Mrs. Wilson was dying
of cancer, I went to her house and grabbed her stuff

in my own vehicle. And how about the kids
I've taught about the outdoors,
sugaring, gardening, helping them stay on the straight
and narrow—even Lamb's kid, for Christ sake."

"Stay away from Justin Lamb, please. His mom's the town
crier shouting twenty-four-seven about the bus
he and his friends are painting in her driveway
and how you're turning these kids into lazy, psychedelic,
pot-smoking hippies. With what's going down
between you and Mickey on account of Justin, it looks
self-serving and vengeful for you rat him out with an old
violation regardless that he filled wetlands and lied about it."
"I'm just telling those kids harmless stories from a past
seemingly so distant they probably imagine dinosaurs."
"Mickey's ex sees you as a malevolent mix
of Wavy Gravy and Ken Kesey."
"They were into sixties music and clothes long before
climbing the landfill fence and meeting me.
Sure, they've probably toked some weed, but so do most kids
from jocks to Goths. Never mentioned it to me."
"Don't you think stories about that nut-job wild-man Sandoz
with his crazy laugh, beat up Chevy, roadkill appetite,
and commune crashing might stir their imaginations?"
"You remember?"
"How could I forget? You had me entranced. I know exactly
what attracts those kids. There's salvation in knowing
an ordinary teenager from our run-of-the-mill town
could stumble into such adventures."
"So you want me to recite them nursery rhymes?"

"Sandoz's story isn't even your best stuff. Tell them about
that elderly Kansas couple that treated you like their son."
"It'll bore them to tears. Too sappy."
"Not if you tell it the way you told me. Over the years,
I've often thought about them as I've sat here quietly solving
people's every day problems, how those simple folks living in
a tiny trailer had heart enough to take care of a young

stranger. It's sweet and humane, and if it doesn't resonate
with them now, I know it will, some day."

"Why did we ever split up?"
"We were kids and we were stupid, I guess. Like I said,
maybe we thought we could do better."
"And again, we never did.
After the shine I took to you, all else left me tarnished."
"Yeah, but that didn't stop you from looking around."
"A little bit," I shrugged. "But it didn't mean nothing."
"That's a double negative."
"You must hear that a lot in politics."
"The world's different when it's all springtime and potential."
"I guess I thought we'd always get back together,
but I also thought I'd go cross country again, be a vagabond,
a Woody Guthrie riding-the-rails traveler."
"After a fashion we've always been together,
just not the way we thought."
The phone rang. "Don't worry, I'm outta here."
"Caleb, maybe we can turn your sugaring operation
and your shack and the whole damn dump into a nature preserve
and environmental center. Think about it."
She handed me back the envelope. I blew her a kiss.

ABUNDANCE SHARED

The file felt lighter as I left town hall, my stomach
still knotted. I'd imagined leaving with a solution,
but just seeing Beryl put me at ease, made me feel grounded,
as if unveiling my secret, mere talk, took some of the weight
from the leaden papers. I'd hoped she'd have an answer,
decide to make it a campaign centerpiece or with a nod
and wink take the envelope, slip it into her desk
and tell me not to worry. Instead, it was locked back
in my Airstream cabinet where several times a day
during breaks I'd take out my precious,
count the pages and run my hands over the blood spattered
print. I was torn between ripping it up and sending
it to everyone from the *Courant* to the *Penny Saver*
and letting the chips fall. Instead, I was a grown
man with a good luck charm, a miser counting out his gold
and looking at his reflected image. I felt filthy, craved
a shower after every time, but couldn't help myself.

Well into harvest season, picking vegetables was my salvation
distraction. For years I gave away zucchini and summer
squash, bushels of tomatoes, eggplants and peppers
to some of my regular patrons. After all, how much
could I eat? It was more connection to the land I craved,
even in the shadow of this strange mound, a wasteland

made productive like the Israelis their blooming Negev.
Some at first refused, thinking food from the dump
contaminated, but they usually took the produce
when I explained it grew in the most carefully tested soil
in town. For months afterward I had meals I'd grown.
At first I cooked fresh casseroles chock full of peas and corn,
ratatouille, lima beans with butter, kale stir-fried with garlic,
acorn and blue Hubbard squash. Latter it was baggies
and plastic containers filled with frozen delights like string
beans with sliced almonds, or carrots soaked in maple syrup.

A few days after I visited Beryl, the boys were back
after school, handing out leaflets with smiles
and helping folks unload their trash, carrying old televisions
and computers to the e-waste trailer and pouring mayonnaise
jars full of crankcase oil into the funnel atop the bung
of a half submerged two-hundred-seventy-five gallon tank.
I caught up on paperwork while they played ambassadors,
peeking out the window occasionally, making sure
vehicles displayed their windshield stickers.
"You got real cheerful, hard workers," a charmed
Alice Evans, an ancient second grade teacher
at Westmoreland Primary School, said to me when I went out
to clear yet another clog in the antiquated compactor.
"And so good to see former students interested in politics,"
she smiled, momentarily stretching smooth her wrinkles.
"I'll bet you won't be too sad to see this smelly
old place go. I'm retiring next year and can't wait.
Love that cruise ship coffee."

At the stroke of three I swung the chain link gate closed
and waited as the boys unloaded black plastic bags
and a couple boxes of bottles and papers from the trunks
of two last vehicles, pulling it open with a smile and wave
as the cars left with faces I knew well, their names unknown
though they knew mine. With the last out I locked up,
the boys having parked just outside the fence as I'd asked.

Now the electioneering posse hurried toward me.
"So how's the campaign," I shouted as they approached.

"Great!" Ronny said. "We've been to Little League
games, the library, and all the stores in town."
"Spent all Saturday in front of the IGA," Billy said.
"After wrestling practice I went up to Rogan's Mill
and he gave me a couple gallons of cider
to give away in small cups just for putting his sign
next to our table with all the cool free stuff."
"Yeah," chimed Ralph, "like pot holders and pencils, jar grips
and chip clips. We brought some stuff for you,"
he said, reaching into a canvass bag that held leaflets
and handing me a couple campaign pencils
and a pouch to hold an I-phone on a dashboard.
"Can we put up a couple posters here?"
"Sorry. Not on town property."
"Told you," Ronny said. "Same thing at the library."
"Well, it didn't hurt to ask. Like dude, Mr. D. is one
of us. He might have different rules."
Ronny rolled his eyes and let out a whistle.
"But the best thing," Justin said, his voice
rising with excitement, "is that we're registering kids at the
high school. A bunch turned 18 over the spring and summer.
We got Mr. Reichert, the principal, to call a special assembly
for seniors and the registrar of voters
came down to swear them in." I couldn't help smiling.
"You guys are amazing," I said. And then, though it felt like
a sour hiccup, "I hope your dad appreciates it, Justin."
"Well, he's still a little sore about the bus, but he knows
we're a big help. Besides, we're kicking butt for the planet."
"If McCarthy had us," Ronny said, "he would have won."

"But the bus! Yeah the bus! That's what we really
wanted to tell you about," Justin said. "You'll be so proud.
It's all brightly colored 'cause after we raided our parents'
basements for half used paint, we went over to Ace Hardware

and got some old spray cans with ripped labels and missing
caps they had lying around. It looks way psychedelic
with silver, blue, green, orange. It's got a rainbow,
and this awesome big peace sign painted on the back.
And not to copy Kesey, but we named it 'Onward,' instead
of 'Further,' written in silver right across the front and . . . ."
"But it's not the outside that's the coolest," big Ralph
interrupted. "Like dude, wait till you step on board.
It's awesome! We took out all the seats
except the driver's and first row and threw down
that Persian rug we found at the swap shack
and strung LED lights all around."
"Yeah, it's like a little living room," Ronny squeaked, "real
cozy with bean bag chairs and a couple of hammocks we can
string up quickly if we need to catch a few zees."
"It's a peaceful place with prayer flags and a couple guitars
for us to fool around with," Justin added.
"Sounds cool," I said, forcing a smile. "Can't wait to see it."
"We'll bring it by as soon as the brakes get done," Billy said.
"They're a bit squishy. But even now it's a sweet place just
to hang, listen to tunes and shoot the shit."
"Like you know," Justin added, "my Mom and Dad
aren't happy, but it's too bad because it's not about them."
With the dayglow bus about to run around town
I knew Mickey Lamb would be back at me, and I was glad
Justin was testing a new found defiance, like a freshly fledged
bird checking out its wings. Still, as a copycat relic the bus
embarrassed me a bit, reminding me of a day when so much
self-inflated silliness masqueraded as serious social
consciousness. It seemed like some spectral archetype
from a naïve world where the slightest action or object
glowed with allegorical significance, yet all it amounted
to was a pseudo Renaissance fair on wheels.
Regardless, I thought, the kids
were having fun and mostly out of harm's way.

"We gotta go," Billy said. "I got practice in 15 minutes."
"Dude, you always got practice," Ronny complained.

"Just chillax. It's, like, the season," Billy replied.
"Before you go," I said, "swing around the garden.
I just picked a couple boxes of vegetables. Take some home
to your parents. Tell them the neon eggplant
and the Cherokee Purple tomatoes are to die for.
Weird colors, but the flavor's out of this world."
"Okay, but after handing out these new brochures tomorrow,"
Justin said, holding a pamphlet with Lamb's nauseatingly
smiling face, "we're going to help you in the garden."
I waved him off. "Not necessary."
"It is for us," Justin insisted to chorusing agreement.
"But we'll want a story," Ronny said in his squeaky nasal
voice that couldn't help sounding like a whine.
"I don't have any more stories. Fresh out."
"Sure you do," Justin said, and then almost pleading, "please."
"There no good ones left, at least."
"Don't blow smoke up our butts, Mr. D.," Billy said. "We
know what's going down, that some of our folks,
especially Justin's dad, aren't too hot on having us hanging
here, but we know you gotta still have some stories
from that trip left and we want to hear them,
especially now that we'll be driving that bus around."
"Although not too far," Ronny added,
"on seven miles a gallon."
"At least tell us when you last saw Sandoz,"
 Ralph said. "That must've been real chill."
"Okay, okay I'll think about it."

HARVEST TIME

The boys were back at two-thirty
the next day handing out those smiling Lamb pamphlets.
Watching from the Airstream, I saw Beryl was right.
The kids were the heartbeat of her opponent's ground game,
their engaging innocence and energy got people to press
the refresh button on Lamb. How I wanted to teach that bully
a lesson. But exposing him was no sure thing and could hurt
Justin, as my friend the first selectman knew. Maybe the boys
would keep him honest and make him hew to his promises.
How could they let him lie after investing so much
of themselves? Wouldn't Lamb risk losing his son forever
if he went back on his pledge to the planet?
I wanted to be out there as little as possible
while they buttonholed for the bastard, so I sat
at my computer and ordered more soil for cover
(from a company controlled by Lamb) and wrote an RFP
for hand tools to replace what was lost, worn, or broken.
Unable to concentrate, I found myself pouring over
my precious, wondering again what to do, embarrassed
by my obsession as if I were online leering at porno.

Soon we were hoeing weeds and harvesting the garden.
I showed Billy and Ralph how to judge a ripe tomato by color
and feel and to toss the rain bloated splits. The eggplants

were glossy and deep purple, the peppers like hanging fists
glowing green. Ronny and Justin chopped weeds
and tossed them on the compost while the others continued
picking. "My mom loved the vegetables and told me to make
sure I thanked you," Ronny said. "The tomatoes reminded
her of her dad's garden when she was a girl. She really
got into it and spent an hour on a big nostalgia trip
about my grandfather, who died when I was four."
They all chimed in with the "thank yous" their parents
had instructed, and I hoped that like Ronny's mom,
these vegetable plot moments would stay with them and buoy
their futures. Gardens were as much about harvesting
memory as produce, and maybe when the boys
came to tell stories of "back in the day," this would be among
them. "Mom said you were way too generous,"
Ronny continued, "and she's giving some to the food bank."
I smiled. "Wow! Great Idea!"

"Holy shit!" Billy said. "Look at the size of this zucchini—
like a baseball bat!" He raised it to his shoulder
like a Louisville Slugger and instinctually swung
when Ralph tossed a tomato that splattered the rest
of us with red juice and seeds. Justin swore
and then we all broke into laughter. Ralph tossed another
couple, one a swing and miss, before I put a stop to it.
"Don't play with your food,"
Ronny scolded with hands on hips, imitating his mom's voice.

"So Mr. D.," Justin said. "We have a question.
We need to think of something to do with the bus.
At first we were heading to Drop City,
but checked it out online and it's long gone."
"I could've told you that."
"So we surfed up a bunch of communes on the web—
they're like mostly called intentional communities, cohousing
and collectives now. We're sweet on the ones with organic
gardening like you're into, and some are big
on beehives and do forestry. We Googled

Ecovillage at Ithaca, Plan B Organic Farm
up in Canada, and an egalitarian place called Acorn
Community in Virginia that has an old-timey
seed business selling some of those weird
colored vegetables you like . . ."
"And there was Dancing Rabbit in Missouri, Earthaven
in North Carolina, and a whole lot more," Ronny
said. "I'd like to visit them all and then decide which one."
"Not going to happen," Ralph said in an Eeyore voice.
"They're a long way off and no way we could keep
the tank filled with the bus' shitty gas millage."
"There'd be major league hassles with our parents," Ronny
added. "Besides, Billy's a senior heading to college on the
left coast next September and we want to do it together."
"With an athletic scholarship to Oregon State," Billy said.
"Wow! Great wrestling school."
"Anyway," Justin said, "we want to do something good
with bus. I mean it's a great hangout
and all, but we want a real purpose."
"What about my idea," Ronny said mischievously.
"Oh yeah, numb-nuts over there wants to make
it my Dad's official campaign bus."
"All the big operations have them."
"Right," Justin shot back, rolling his eyes. "Dad would go off
like a nuclear bomb. Anyway," he turned back to me, "help
us try to come up with something. We don't want people to
see just some stupid teen hang out and dumb toy."

"How 'bout that story you promised," Ronny said.
"You've heard the best ones, and I didn't say for sure."
"My mom bets you got hundreds, but not to believe it all."
"Yeah, another about Sandoz," Justin insisted.
Again, I was tempted to get at Lamb and all the back biting gossipers
by spinning some stoner revel or giggly acid trip that made
everything more than it was, halos and shimmering auroras,
steep and dizzy. Or maybe I could reminisce
about the VW microbus ride with a dope smoking couple
who pulled into a McDonalds parking lot for an orgy.

But I couldn't use the kids to get at Lamb, however tempting.
Maybe Beryl was right. I'd tell them about the elderly couple,
little older than I was now, who seduced me with deepest
kindness no matter that I belonged to the "class of the bad
attitude" drunk on Kerouac's beatitude
at a time when respectable elders were expected to steer
clear of long hair and bell bottoms. "I'll tell you about some
of the coolest people I ever met, but I bet you'll be bored.
They were better than cool, welcomed a stranger,
taught me for real how people should be treated."

CARPENTER

Leaving Sunshine House and standing on Denver's Federal
Avenue ramp bound at last for home, the road was thick
with traffic. Only ten minutes and I thought luck was mine
with three cars pulling over. But one was connecting
with I-25 south toward Pueblo, the other two
taking I-70. Aiming for 76 north, I wanted to catch
I-80 up in Wyoming and ride a more northerly route east.
Eager to see new country and faces, I'd make the return trip
different. After nearly a month on the road
I was an old hand, knew where I was going.

Another fifteen minutes and an old man in a beat up station
wagon pulled over in front of me, motioning with his hand
out the window. The car was dragging ass and a bit lopsided
suggesting shot shocks and a heavy load. "I want 80 east,"
I yelled over a muffler rat-tat-tatting like a machine gun.
I couldn't hear a word, but he nodded and leaned
over to unlock the passenger door. The car rolled a bit
as his foot pulled off the brake and I hopped in.
"Hello! How's it going!" I sounded like a cheerleader,
some of that western happy-to-know-you-attitude at last
veneering my native reserve. He tipped his painter's cap.
"Good, Good. And You?" he asked with a smile
and slight drawl.

*For the first time in weeks there weren't mountains
in front of me and I turned a few times for a backward
glance over the concrete tongue leading toward the rucked,
jagged 3D of the Rockies. Flatlands ahead were crowded
with houses and as I gazed to the endless horizon,
I caught in the corner of my eye a giant steel sign
with the red, white and blue I-70 shield. My stomach tensed
as if readying for a punch and I felt slightly car sick. The fork
to I-76 went by and disappeared. We'd missed the turn!*

*"You sure you want I-70?" I asked, in a dry-throated
tremulous voice. "Yup. Still the way back
to Kansas. Least I hope so," he chuckled.
A momentary quiet seemed to stretch into the distance.
I clenched my teeth so hard my jaw ached.
"It's okay for you, ain't it?" he wondered sympathetically.
I tried holding the tremble in my voice. "Yeah, sure."
I could've had him pull over and let me run across the median
to hitch back to the big "Y" of concrete where the roads split.
He could've let me off at an exit for a state route
heading north so I could catch I-80 in Wyoming, but back
roads here were tough for copping rides
and I didn't feel like standing hungry in the hot, dry sun
for hours. With the muffler as loud as a lawnmower,
he must have misunderstood my destination.
I-70 was the road I'd taken on my way out, but maybe
it would look different in reverse. And this old coot
was no Sandoz. The trip had a life of it's own
I couldn't fight and wrong turns couldn't ruin it.
There were no wrong turns.*

*Staring out the window while the old fellow
kept to his driving, I gazed at acre upon acre of fields rolling
to the horizon with occasional depressions
that made the treeless land appear even more table-like.
Houses, roads, and villages were all at a precise ninety
degrees. With few distinctions, everything was queerly
familiar so that miles seemed to lose meaning,*

each place offering the eye the same enticements.
Although I'd been through before, I recognized nothing,
and only rotating odometer numbers
and road signs bespoke progress.

"By the way," he said, after not quite half an hour
of quiet, "I'm Carl. Hail from Grinnell in Kansas.
Know where that is?" I shook my head. "It's ways east
of Oakley, not far from the Colorado line."
Glancing at me and rubbing a stubble gray chin,
he added, "guess that's not much help, huh."
I laughed, shaking loose the last tension
that hadn't seeped out in the miles.

"Where 'bouts you from? My grandson's always warnin'
me not to give his friends the third degree,
sos if you don't feel like answering, just say so.
But you do kind of remind me of Tommy, what with long hair
and everything. Don't care for it myself, but the wife keeps
telling me he's clear old enough to make such decisions
and I suppose she's right, mostly. Usually is. But it don't
matter the getups he wears and all, he's a good boy and darn
smart. Must get it from his grandma. We raised him since
he was eight after my daughter and her husband were killed
by a drunk driver." A nervous laugh escaped his lips.
"Sorry. Don't mean to chew your ear off."

He had a wide smile, shiny gold tooth sparkling
on the side of his mouth, a penetrating smile, a smile
that loosened me, a Fred MacMurray "My Three Sons"
type grin that was real. It was nothing like the Jesus freak
stagey smiles of Sunshine House. I didn't feel like talking, yet
words flowed easily and suddenly I was bursting
with questions, discovering that he'd just dropped
his grandson off for some summer program at the university
in Boulder. "He's going for some kind of engineering. Forget
which one exactly, but it was hard to get into. I know that."

*He had an odd manner of speaking.
He'd start slow in a kind of stutter and then, after a few
difficult words, as if he'd gotten himself wound up, he'd talk
rapidly and clearly for a few sentences before slowing down
and beginning the cycle again. As he spoke, a corner
of his lip hung loose and swayed slightly as if the muscle
had died. Otherwise, he was a handsome man with wide
shoulders, a reddish complexion and shock of white hair.*

*After we got through the usual where and what, I thought
the conversation would die, but we kept talking
like it was a backyard barbecue. He didn't get past tenth
grade, and as a kid shoveled grain for slave wages
in a Wichita elevator. There were snowy miles
walked to school, fishing, shooting cans off a fence
with a .22 rifle and the Model A that was his first ride.
We talked baseball, and he was sure Willie Mays
would beat out the Babe for most round trippers some day.*

*A half retired carpenter (close to Jesus his wife said),
the back seat was down and the wagon's rear
cluttered with saws and saw horses, clamps, hammers,
a long level, wrenches and chisels. A couple drill bits
rolled around the floor at my feet, banging occasionally
on a rusty plane. The car smelled of sawdust and machine
oil. "What with the boy in college on a good scholarship I
don't have to break my back anymore. At least
that's what Sue tells me, and she does the finances.
Just take occasional jobs that are interesting and pay
well, like cabinet work." The miles weren't so empty
when the landscape was filled with a man and stories.*

*"I love this here country. Lots of folks having their first trip
on through say it's boring, but not to me. A man
has his distance out here. Don't feel crowded in by nothing,
and the sun rises and sets something fiercely beautiful.
Nowhere to hide. An honest place."
As we drove, soft fluffy clouds gathering on the horizon*

*grew to giant charcoal monsters. "We're in for a real
thumper," he said as they drew closer, stirring the wind
and darkening the countryside. Sun shone
from behind the inky mass like theater lights, and to the north
and south we spied the storm's edge. Timpani rumbles
of thunder echoed and a jagged lightning arrow
pierced the electrically charged clouds
that looked like heavenly mountains. Sky suddenly seemed
the heavier element, as if the world had flipped. Bullets
of rain pelted us, banged the roof and hood. In five minutes it
was over, Panzer divisions of grim clouds rolling
on, thunder reverberating in the growing distance as the road
steamed and dried in sunshine.*

PLAIN FOLKS
ON THE PLAINS

Late in the day, the old man braked gently for his exit.
"How 'bout joining me and the wife for dinner,"
he smiled, gold tooth gleaming. "We ain't got much,
but we'd sure be proud to have you." I hesitated.
"Nah, I don't want to impose," came the automatic polite
response drilled into me since childhood,
though I ached with hunger and hoped he'd repeat the offer.
"Oh, hell. Don't mind that. I know folks
done it for Tommy. No other way to repay
them than by offering to a stranger."
I felt wanted, like the invitation wasn't for my benefit
alone. I flashed a big grin and nodded.

Coasting off the interstate, we did a few paved miles
and turned onto twin rutted tracks separated by a line of dry
grass which swooshed against the undercarriage. The wagon
bucked and shook on potholes and hard packed
washboarded earth. From a slight rise, we descended
to a cluster of trailer homes, their white and silvery skins
sparkling even in the low angled late day
sunlight where half a dozen faced each other like circled
wagons. A couple large elms hung over the dusty courtyard
they created. We pulled up to a long white structure
with yellow trim and shutters. Grass green plastic carpeting

*covered the steps on either side of clay pots
in which petunias bloomed. A horse stood lazily
tethered to a wooden post. Somehow I'd imagined him living
in a big old white farmhouse. The trailer
seemed too modern, confining and transient.*

*"Sue! Sue!" he bellowed, the screen door slamming
behind us. "I've got a young guest with me."
We entered a living room furnished with thick, darkly stained
pine furniture. A small braided rug lay in front of a coffee
table graced with copies of* Time *and* Readers' Digest.
*An old jug fitted as a lamp rested on an end table.
"How nice to meet you," came Sue's high pitched voice
as she entered from the combination kitchen and dining area.
Sue was thin, but not frail, with a delicate nose, deep brown
eyes and full bosom. She wore a flowery house dress
with an apron and fuzzy yellow slippers.
"I hope it's okay," I said.
"Not to worry so long as you don't mind that the place
is a mess. Carl's forever bringing home guests.
I almost plan for it. We've got plenty." She gave me a quick
look. "Not from this area, are you?"*

*"Mother, can't you see the boy's hungry. Don't pester
him with a million and one questions. He's from back east,
a few years younger than Tom and going to college in the fall.
Now you know all there's a need for before we eat."
Sue put hands on her hips. "Pshaw Carl. I wasn't pestering.
No way. Let the feller speak for himself, for land sakes."
Carl went to the fridge and offered me a beer and Sue
asked how old I was, quickly giving into Carl's claim
that I was "growed enough" to drink baby brew.
"Always buy the 3.2 beer. Like the taste, but don't want it
going to my head," he said. Carl and I sat
in front of a nineteen inch Admiral with rabbit ears
while Sue set the table and watched the macaroni
and cheese casserole in the oven.*

"Okay boys. Come and git it!"
She called us like she was rounding up cowhands.
"Have mercy, Mother. Cronkite ain't done yet."
She teased with a scolding finger.
"Tell him to wrap it up. I'll give him five minutes."

A steaming Pyrex dish sat in the middle of the table
while we had cantaloupe and then salad with cukes, tomatoes,
onions and peppers. The mac and cheese was chewy
and cheesy with a coating of crunchy crust.
"Now come on, son, have some more,"
Sue insisted after I'd wolfed down two large portions.
"Thanks, but I'm pretty full," I said, patting my stomach.
Sue shook her head. "Look at you! Just skin and bones.
Probably haven't had a decent meal since you saw your ma
last. I'll bet she's worried sick," she said, scraping
the last of the casserole onto my plate.
"Why don't you use our phone. She'd be so glad to hear
from you. In fact, when your done eating you go
into the bedroom and pick up the Princess on the night
stand. We won't hear a thing."

"You remind me so much of Tom," Sue went on, "and his
appetite is just as fine. Makes it a pleasure to cook.
He's all we got, Pa and me, since his mom and dad
were killed by that New Year's eve drunk in Lincoln
where his father was lawyering for the state senate.
Rolled down an embankment and squished the Ford beyond
recognition. Tommy was eight then, home with a sitter,
thank the Lord. Ever since, we've raised him ourselves.
It ain't been easy at our age, but it's been a blessing."

With the busyness of food and clearing and cleaning dishes
and conversation Sue didn't remind me to call Mom
and I wasn't going to bring it up. I didn't want to break
the spell. For once I enjoyed being a son. And soon
we were all on the couch looking at family photos
and pictures Tommy had taken of farmhouses

and Denver skyscrapers. Some of the images
were kind of neat, though listening to them carry on got a bit
dull. Still, just sharing pictures that meant so much
to them was fun. Strangely, the room filled with the same vibe
as passing around the water-filled whiskey bottle at Drop.

When we'd been through most of the pictures,
Sue asked if I wanted anything more,
though I didn't know what "more" could possibly be.
"Thanks much, but I'm really full."
She smiled, her face stretching and briefly hinting
at the much younger woman years had left behind.
"Not too full for homemade apple pie a la mode,
I'll bet you're not."
She was right. I had room for that.

Carl reminisced over coffee, his face glowing even brighter
with the warmth. "Things have worked out pretty good.
This here trailer ain't much, but its home,"
he drawled, patting a dark wood panel. "Damn sturdy,
too. Making them better all the time."
He sighed, that hanging piece of lip slightly trembling,
his eyes widening and then closing slowly. A cloudy moment
of hound-dog sadness seemed to pass through him
and I wondered about things I could never know.
Suddenly a smile stole across his face. "Amazing how notions
have changed since I was your age," he said, shaking
his head slowly. "Used to be people took meals indoors
and went out to the one holer. Nowadays folks have dinner
on an outdoor patio and go inside to flush."

I finished a second cup of coffee and before I could put
it down Sue offered another. "Thanks, but I want
to try a couple more rides before dark, so I should hit
the road." A worried mother look stole over her face.
"Why don't you rest up for the evening, sit and watch
the ballgame with me and set out tomorrow bright
and early after breakfast," Carl suggested with his warm,

gold tooth smile. Sue clasped her hands.
Perfect! We won't have it any other way."
I begged off twice again before they gave up. After all
their arguments of rest, food, dangers on the road
after dark, and a soft bed, I swayed
them with the disappointment of friends should I get home
later than planned. In fact, no one was expecting
me by a certain day, but being with them had made
me homesick, oddly enough driving me away
from the comfort of their embrace.

Sue "lardered" me up with two ham and cheese sandwiches,
a couple peaches and a baggie of carrot sticks.
She made me promise not to hitch after dark, and handed
me flashlight batteries. As we pulled away, she waved sadly
from the door. The bottom of the sun was about to be clipped
by the horizon when I stepped from the rattletrap wagon.
"You been good company, son. Hope you get a quick ride."
After unloading my gear, I leaned back into the car for a firm
handshake, and when we parted I was holding six dollars.
"I can't take this."
He smiled. "Sure you can. They ain't that heavy, you know."
"Really. You've given me so much already."
"Look, when my boy's been trying to hitchhike a ride
I know folks have been good to him. How else can I pay
them back." Stuffing the bills in my pocket, he grinned.
I slammed the rusty door and the car U turned.
I walked up the ramp, a long, faint shadow in front of me.

GHOSTS FUTURE

Dog-eared, yellowed and brittle with age and a cracked
binding hemorrhaging pages, I found the indispensable
"access to tools" on a swap shack shelf
paperweighted by a bicentennial commemorative plate
and a baseball glove. Reading the seductive Whole Earth oath
that "we are as gods and might as well get good at it,"
I surfed the paper internet for yurt and log cabin designs;
instructions in falconry, natural childbirth,
shoe retreading, and dairy goat husbandry; sources for auto
parts, helicopters, pumps, pipes, hand printing presses,
windmills, and primitive computers;
guidance on telescopes, woodstoves, houseboats, stereo
systems, psychic discoveries, and communes. L.L. Bean
for the hip and restless, I found a magic carpet collage
of discarded expectations, vicarious
aspirations, and sweet, gullible innocence. Haunted
by possibilities, I seemed to have released the stale air
of a long buried time capsule
whose beguiling pieces of the past still shone shiny new.

TOBACCO INDUSTRY PLEDGES
BROADCAST BAN IN 1970

On August 1st the world becomes a happier
place to fly on TWA

COLUMBUS RIOTING BRINGS OUT GUARD

The promoters of a rock music festival in Wallkill, N.Y. met yesterday to plan security

Remember what the dormouse said

COME TO WHERE THE FLAVOR IS:
COME TO MARLBORO COUNTRY

the good old days when only God could end the world.

75 PROTESTORS HELD AT ILLINOIS CAPITOL

All the lonely people, where do they all come

ABM FIGHT TAKEN TO SENATE FLOOR

Like a bird on a wire, like a drunk

RETURN TO SENDER

Maybe I bored them to sleep or they slipped into a fugue,
but the boys stayed for the story as it dragged long past dark.
Not the most engaging tale or the first thing the sixties
brought to mind, but Beryl was right. It probably
had the most profound and longest lasting effect on me.
While other tales were fun and amusing, here I felt strangely
warmed in the telling. Among all the tie dye, drugs, loud
guitars, defiant lifestyles, hip talk and wanderlust
were an ordinary couple who'd made me at home thousands
of miles from where I lived. Maybe I stayed at the landfill
so long because of them, because this is where I'd get to meet
regular folks who made me feel good, not just glad-handers
chatting me up about getting ahead or the latest fashion.
People talked about life's basics at the dump
because what was more ordinary, unglamorous
and yet necessary than tossing trash. It might sound
saccharin to those hiding behind the ironic poses that shelter
so many today, but on the Kansas flatlands
I'd discovered you could unexpectedly find deep
connections with an empathetic ear and knowing voice
that gave meaning to superficial niceties.
Hundreds of people poured through my gate every week
and I was the welcoming committee, each day
repaying Carl and Sue for their kindness.

After the boys were gone and well past dinnertime,
I went to my desk to turn off the computer only to see Lamb's
shit-eating grin staring at me from a pile of pamphlets the kids
had left. For a while I'd forgotten the thin, incriminating file
that seemed at times to fill a drawer, the cabinet,
the whole room. I felt the walls get close, the air warm
and thicken, and though I was starving and eager to get back
to the cabin, the temptation to gaze
again at the pages was irresistible. I grabbed the key
from under the turtle shell and pulled the envelope gingerly,
sliding out the papers as if they were stovetop hot.
I couldn't stand to keep them anymore,
my obsession worsening, hearing Lamb's voice in the words
on the pages like a tell-tale heartbeat. Election day
was but a few weeks away and I needed to make a decision
or one would be made by doing nothing.
Alternatives had seethed, boiled in me for weeks,
and now whistled in my ear like a steaming teakettle.

Could I really defeat Lamb by sending his emails
to the media? Maybe Beryl was right and he'd get sympathy
for what seemed a classic October surprise, a Nixonian
trick. And if the statute of limitations had passed,
would it be just an empty, even vengeful gesture. No frontal
assault would do. I couldn't simply threaten
going to the media. It'd be seen as self serving, and Lamb
might even claim political blackmail. Still,
something had to give. I couldn't keep the documents
any longer or they would make me crazy—
insects buzzing in ever rising decibels

Was it my better angels I was wrestling?
 I couldn't tell beyond reasonable doubt. Crazy
thoughts ghosted through me like a chill winter wind.
Did Lincoln or Jacob really know which angels they tussled
with? I couldn't just toss the documents into the recycling bin.
Who was I to veto what voters had a right to know?
I read and reread, thumbed the corners, rolled the papers,

smoothed them and curled them again, pacing in my mind
like a stereotyped expectant father in the hospital hallway.

Pushing midnight, I made my decision though ripe
with doubt. Addressing them to Lamb, I trifolded
the documents and on a yellow sticky note
wrote that I'd found them blown across the pavement
and caught against the fence. I thought he'd want them back,
I wrote, and then, almost as a dig, wished him luck
in the election. It was a slight and subtle message without
threatening or recrimination, but I couldn't resist.
If someone had asked, I would have said that I meant
bad luck. Lamb was savvy, would get the message.
The point would be made, communication complete,
and I'd be done with restless dreams, the daily
weighing of alternatives. Maybe the implicit
message would cause him to back off,
tone things down even if he didn't change course.

Ready to seal the deal and lick the number ten
envelope, I checked that the address was correct to a company
box. With no return designation and stamp affixed,
I withdrew the documents once more, a last glance
at my precious and proud that I was able to part.
But in a sudden burst of fear, sense of power, or desire
for possession I looked one last time and took
them to the copier. Suspicious Lamb would assume
I'd kept a duplicate, so why not? A copy would not keep
me up, buzz or boil or beat like an irregular heart,
and if it did, only as a faint shadow of the blood spattered
original. One to the file, one to the mailbox, I powered down
the machines, went home to a meal of canned soup and two
bottles of Bud and fell into the deepest sleep in weeks.

TRUCK

Almost a week since the envelope was stamped and sealed
and I'd heard nothing from Lamb. I'd expected a fire siren
scream after no more than a couple days since
a well-run campaign wouldn't let the daily delivery
sit on a desk. Candidates had to respond to queries
and sometimes there were checks waiting to be cashed.
Lamb had to be up to something and over the past
few days I'd moved with a nervous energy, listening more
carefully than usual to conversations while folks unloaded,
looking over my shoulder occasionally at a diesel's rumble.
I didn't think he'd go to the cops, but there might
be surveillance on the QT. Sixties style paranoia crept over
me like in college years when we'd wander tightly
clenched and wasted into town, finding ourselves at a late
night eatery red-eyed and giggling, sure that everyone knew.
Was he calling my bluff, figuring an old-line
peacenik was just puffing and would never pull the trigger?
Or he could be taking the offensive, going to the media
and readying them for wild and false accusations
from me or anonymous sources. Maybe he just didn't give
a crap and was waiting for me to make the next move.
Sending the stuff provided relief at first,
but now I was as jumpy as ever, the copies
beginning to cast the same spell, assume the same power
over me as the originals. What had I expected?

The boys had been back a couple days earlier
passing out more leaflets. I winced with each one placed
in a patron's hand, one more step to the first
selectman's office for Lamb. At closing, they came
to the gate while I locked up. "Good news!"
Justin said. "Dad had the bus towed down
to Goodhall's Garage and he's paying to fix it."
"Yeah, dude" Ralph whistled, "and the bill's gonna come
to over five Franklins! Needs a new master cylinder
and some lines, rotors and stuff."
Justin nodded. "It's not that he likes the bus or anything,
and he said we can't use it for campaigning.
Still, he's grateful for all the work we're doing."
"Sounds good," I said indifferently,
though in their excitement I don't think they noticed.
Beryl was probably right again, and Lamb's bus cash
was a bribe to win over his son.

A typically slow midweek day with lots of leaf loads
for the compost as folks cleared their lawns with October
coming to a close. I had several small Everests of ragged
brown foliage, and their pungent earthy smell in the cool
air overwhelmed the garbage, a sure sign
of the season, the planet creaking on its axis.
At this time of year, residents rushing with their rakings,
I often kept the place open a few minutes extra,
and it was 3:20 when I let out the last vehicle, a pickup
with the back and sides built up by sheets of plywood
to maximize a fluffy load. I locked the gate and walked
to the dozer to spread soil on the day's deliveries of trash.

About to climb into the Deere, I turned to a crashing
and scratchy high pitched wrench of metal on metal as a Ford
F-350 flatbed with twin vertical exhaust stacks and gleaming
diamond plate burst through the gate sending half of it flying
and the rest under the tires. I stood frozen as the big diesel
with dual rear wheels roared toward me like an angry
animal. Painted gray with a familiar triangular logo

on the door, I knew it was Mickey Lamb
though his face was obscured by windshield reflected
sunlight. Showing no sign of slowing as it came closer,
I dodged to the right and the truck swerved toward
me, the grill gleaming like the maw of some science fiction
monster. Was he trying to run me down?
I couldn't believe he was chasing me. I turned
again, and with the bumper a foot away I ducked
between a compactor and the scrap metal rolloff.
The truck came to a screeching halt and from behind the bin
I saw a cloud of dust rising. The engine grumbled at idle
and I heard the door open. "Come out you sniveling coward,
or I'm coming to get you. You think you can threaten me?
You don't have the balls to go to the papers."
I stayed put, my legs rubbery, body shaking.

"I'm coming to get you buddy, and it ain't going to be pretty."
I heard footsteps, each one a threatening word, and as soon
as he rounded the side of the steel container I took off,
sprinting for the trailer where I could lock the door and dial
help. His boots pounded on the dusty macadam
and halfway across the yard I could hear his breathing.
I heard a grunt as he must have lunged like in high school
football days. He hit hard, seemed to climb
my back and suddenly I was on the ground, arms and chin
scraping on the gritty sandpapery pavement. He got off me.
"Get up you lousy coward. You think you can ruin
my reputation? Get up or I'll get you up."
Pain and nausea, hot and cold hit me in waves.
He yanked my arms and suddenly I was standing.

"That's better," he said, hands on his hips, his face
that reddened knot, a sneering half smile on his lips.
It took all my effort to stand as the world spun.
"You broken down hippie faggot. Time to fight back."
"I don't want to fight you."
"What? I can't hear you," he taunted.
"I'm not fighting you," I repeated louder.

"You pissant little bastard, you're going to have to."
He stretched out a leg behind me, pushed, and I tripped
backward. "Careful," he said, "you might lose your balance."
He pulled me up again, wobbly and woozy.
"You'll pay for this," I said.

"You going to call the cops?" he jeered.
"Go ahead," he said, reaching into his pocket.
"You can use my cell. The number's 911, in case
you've forgotten. I'll dial, if you want."
I said nothing, putting all my effort into just standing.
"Kosko's on duty and in the cruiser now. I put an addition
on his house a few years back at a very reasonable price.
Let's see. I'll say I saw you fall from the dozer
as I approached, got distracted and accidentally crashed
through the gate. I'm rushing to take you to the E.R.
and get you fixed up, yes that's what I was going to do,
wasn't it. It's a new truck and no one would believe
I'd intentionally dent it. Besides, I'll call my crew
and in about an hour the gate will be like new. It'll be your
word against mine. A broken down garbage
picker against a successful businessman who puts people
to work, donates to causes, and is about to be top dog
in this town. You're just a vengeful little man
afraid I'll pull you off the public tit."

Body beaten with flu-like aches, I began
regaining my balance though the scrapes stung.
"You won't get away with this," was all I could manage.
"You think Beryl is going to pull your nuts out of the fire
this time. She's protected you for years, but that's done.
You still fucking her? I mean nice rack, but time's passed.
I wouldn't tap that if I were paid."
I lunged at him, but stumbled like a drunk.
He sidestepped and I almost fell.
"You think you got it all figured out don't you,"
I said weakly. He smiled.
"You bet I do. It's checkmate, my friend.

And I wasn't born yesterday. Let's go to the trailer.
I want the copies you made."
We both turned to a loud noise that sounded like a bad
muffler. Coming down the maple lined lane,
painted in dayglow orange and yellow was the psychedelic
bus, a disjoint, swirling rainbow on wheels with "Sugar
Magnolia," blossoms blooming, booming out the windows.

BUS

Justin at the wheel, the bus screeched to a stop six feet in front
of us, music suddenly silenced and the boys piling
out like it was on fire. "What happened?"
they asked simultaneously, staring at my bruised body looking
as if I'd fallen down a long flight of stairs, my nose bleeding,
forehead and arms scrapped. With a quick glance
in my direction, Lamb turned to the boys. His voice
was measured and soft, like he was trying to calm a hysterical
friend. "Mr. Dempster had an accident
falling into the scrap metal bin." Again he turned to me,
but I gave no sign of contradiction or trying to speak.
"I was passing by and the dump was closed,
but I saw what happened and broke through the gate to help.
Let's get him to one of those seats in front of the trailer."

"Are you hurt bad?" Ronny squeaked. "We can drive
you to the hospital on the bus."
"There's a mattress in back you can lie on," Justin said.
"It's real comfortable," Ronny added.
Their concern was healing, but I was too dazed
to tell whether they believed Lamb's story.
I didn't have the strength to argue, wasn't sure
what would come of it at the moment.
Lamb was so skilled at bullshitting, and as an adult

with authority, it was hard to know what the boys thought.
Besides, I still had a naïve belief that the truth would come
out, that the whole tawdry mess would backfire on Lamb.
"I think I'm going to be okay after I get cleaned up,"
I said, as the boys helped me onto the avocado toilet
between a gnome that looked like one of Snow White's
dwarfs and the mannequin Beryl claimed wore the wrong bra.
"I just need to catch my breath."

"We have something really cool to tell you,"
Justin said, after I was seated. "We decided on a really sweet
purpose for the bus without heading out to some far off
commune where no one knows us."
Mickey Lamb ambled over like some crazed Wyatt Earp
who'd just proved he's the quickest draw.
"The boys can take you to the walk-in if you need,"
he said, and if I didn't know better I'd have thought
he was really concerned. "I'm going back to the shop.
I'll round up a couple guys and we'll have that gate fixed
in a jiffy. Better than new, I guarantee,"
he said like a salesman. Then in more deliberate tones.
"We're good, right." I acted like I didn't hear him.
"We're good with each other, right Dempster." I nodded.
"Uhuh," was all I said. He turned, walked to his truck
and drove out. I felt a little triumph. I still had the copy,
though I knew now I wasn't going to do anything
with it. Not that I was intimidated, despite Lamb's
considerable intimidation. I was tired of hassling,
and revenge would only make me smell like that skunk
Jack Ellyat warned about. Besides, it wouldn't
make a difference in the election. If it had been
otherwise, I probably would have done something by now.

"You sure we can't take you over to the doc-in-the-box
and get you checked out," Billy asked. "Like dude,
you really don't look so great."
"Not as bad as it looks," I smiled. "Only hurts when I laugh."
"Pretty lame, Mr. D.," Ronny said.

"I'll be fine. Tell me about the bus."
"The brakes are all set and for less than $500 because
the rotors weren't so worn. But now we got this hole in the
muffler. Getting something on EBay
can be dicey. Like, you never know."
I shook my head. "I mean clue me in to your idea,
since you've given up on the commune plan?"

"Actually, it was my mom's idea,"
Ronny said. "Remember all the vegetables you sent home
with us? She didn't have time to freeze them and it was more
than we could eat so she had me bring them down to Food
Share over in Windsor where they have this big warehouse
and send stuff to soup kitchens and food banks all over.
And like, I told her about all the veggies you were growing,
and she said there's too much waste at supermarkets
and farms. I was telling her about the bus
and she didn't think communes were so slick
but what about using it to help hungry people."
"Way cool idea!" I said, with as much gusto as my pounding
head would allow. "Far out, as we used to say."
"It kind of goes with all the stuff we've been doing together,"
Justin said. "You know, like sugaring and growing greens
and radishes and tomatoes in the garden. We'd like to set up
a bin for donated canned goods right here next
to the recycling. Billy's new girlfriend, Rachel, she's an artist
who can make a really cool sign. Is it okay?"
"Consider it done."
"Of course, it's not her art talents that got him to ask her out,"
Ralph quipped. "He was a deer caught in the headlights,
like real big ones." Justin teased.
"Boobs out to here," he gestured as Billy blushed.

"We also thought about how much it meant
to you, having that old Kansas couple feed you when you
were hungry. Everything pointed to helping folks
with food. It just seemed right. The bus gets a real purpose,
whatever else anyone thinks about the colors and psychedelic

shit. Like, this is really a way of bringing people together.
With the election over in a few days," Justin continued,
"we needed a new cause, something else to help change
the world. We're going to set up at libraries and stores
and collect non-perishable foods. Maybe you'll start
seeing less rotting garbage from refrigerators.
We'll go to farms and collect veggies that might
go to waste. Because the bus is different,
we think the curiosity factor will attract
people and then they'll be generous."

"You sure we can't take you to get looked at,"
Billy wondered. "One of your eyes is swelling."
"You got a shiner coming for sure," Ralph said.
"Thanks, I'm okay boys. Why don't you head to the garden
and pick whatever is left. It's been a few days since I've
harvested so there's bound to be a bounty of late crops
you can take over to Windsor—kale, beets, carrots,
and probably a bushel of acorn squash and some blue
Hubbard. Take whatever is good to go. I got plenty back
in the cabin. Let me grab some syrup jugs from the trailer."

"Okay," Justin said, "but first Ronny
has an important question about the 60s."
"Do not!" Ronny protested, his face reddening.
"Sure you do," the others responded in unison
as Billy gave him a friendly shove.
"Whatever you guys want to know. Go ahead and shoot."
Justin took a deep breath. "Ronny wants to know if the babes
in the 60s really went braless."
I smiled, shook my head, and entered the trailer for the syrup.

WATCHING THE RIVER FLOW

Sunday after the election and the dump is quiet as I sit atop
the mountain I've built, my monument to the past, pyramid
of treasure for the future. A rare warm early November
day when you think of spring though winter yaws
ahead like an insuperable chasm. Circled by hills
whose ridges and pinnacles fade to a blue-gray horizon,
I feel a jagged edge to the world. In the near distance, church
spires and town hall's brownstone clock tower poke
above the dendritic fretwork of nearly bare trees.
It's mostly oaks that still have leaves bronzed and coppery,
a burnished landscape. Overhead, turkey vultures
are kettleling, taking advantage of thermals, flapping
and coasting, circling in graceful silhouettes
that belie their repulsive fleshy heads. With telescopic
eyesight, they're looking for rotting road kill or a deer carcass
run by dogs. They are my kin, in the business of taking care
of what's useless and spoiled, cleaning up and recycling.

At ease in the sun, my scrapes and sores healing after I drove
myself to the walk-in clinic and got cleaned up, I never
saw Lamb return with his crew. When I got back, the gate
was repaired and a new lock hung on the hasp with fresh keys
dangling. Of course, he won election by a wide margin
as Beryl had predicted, though I'm glad she's still

on the board. Maybe she's right and I've been
running this landfill too long. I need a kick
in the ass and out of the doldrums spawned by disappointment
so long ago. Still, it's not going to happen quickly.
State environmental staff say the closure plan requires
updating and a park will need several additional approvals.
Could be three years or more to get the place
closed, and by then Beryl's nature center
idea might just be the ticket. Still, I could bag
the whole thing. I'm making up too many reasons to stay.

Some of the communes the boys mentioned are as seductive
as beautiful women. I could recapture a portion
of the world I'd tried to grasp so many years ago.
I liked the education center idea at Earthaven,
and the Southern Exposure Seed Exchange at Acorn,
but felt a real connection to the ones focused on social
sustainability. I want to go forward, and wonder
if they'd be a step back from where I am.
Maybe becoming a Transition Town advocate is the fit,
stirring things up locally about peak oil, organics, anti-toxics
and GMOs where I know the politics and people
and can grow into a gadfly making things hot for politicians
like Lamb. Wouldn't I like to see him sweat,
be roasted even. Beryl says after the honeymoon,
he'll be flattened by conflicting demands and details
and his temper will undo him. It's tempting.

For so long, each moment has been a slow backward glance,
but the boys helped exorcise the demons. I feel so light,
though still uncomfortable. Where once I was confined,
now it's the buffet of alternatives creating a quandary.
Maybe my cross country trip and kindred experiences
weren't so meaningless after all. The boys appeared to thrive
on those stories that seemed so distant, inspired
to find a way to make a difference, at least for now.
I once longed for a tomorrow that never arrived
after a thousand sunsets, but they might get to enjoy the dawn.

After all these years, I still don't know if we can make
a go of it, find a world less violent
and devious, more creative, organic and authentic.
All I know is that I'm starved
for something and I've still got a hungry heart.

The river runs through our town, and if you grew
up here you swam in it, skated on it, fished and messed
around in boats. The town is here because of the river,
because a century-and-a-half ago it supplied
the power to make buttons. We still drink from it upstream
and dispose of our waste below. How few
of us actually look at it carefully, feel it's moods,
see it in four dimensions, in time as well as space.

From here I see a shimmering surface in fishscale patterns
as errant gusts sweep across the water. I seem to fall back
in time, wondering what it was like when this hill
was a swamp and the river the principal artery of travel
for natives floating birchbark so perfect for its purpose
as to be indistinct from the water. Imagine that breathtaking
world inhabited more by spirits and stories
than objects such as fill this mound, things so transitory
and meaningless as to be easily tossed and interred.
I'm not nostalgic, for nostalgia is corrosive,
a longing for an illusory golden age that robs us of hope.
But the world, I'm sure, would be better should each
of us possess at least some transitory enchanted moments
when a slice of that ancient uncluttered world
might be regained to renew our sense of wonder,
myth and mystery, making the present more meaningfully
alive and filled with possibilities. Go with the flow
was a catch phrase of the sixties that caught us short.
I watch the river and learn.

ACKNOWLEDGEMENTS

In gratitude to Rennie McQuilkin, Chivas Sandage, and John Stanizzi, fine poets whose work I admire, for their insightful comments and encouragement in pursing this curious animal of a book.

HOMEBOUND
PUBLICATIONS

At Homebound Publications we recognize the importance of going home to gather from the stores of old wisdom to help nourish our lives in this modern era. We choose to lend voice to those individuals who endeavor to translate the old truths into new context and keep alive through the written word ways of life that are now endangered. Our titles introduce insights concerning mankind's present internal, social and ecological dilemmas.

It is our intention at Homebound Publications to revive contemplative storytelling. We publish full-length introspective works of: non-fiction, essay collections, epic verse, short story collections, journals, travel writing, and novels. In our fiction titles our intention is to introduce new perspectives that will directly aid mankind in the trials we face at present.

It is our belief that the stories humanity lives by give both context and perspective to our lives. Some older stories, while well-known to the generations, no longer resonate with the heart of the modern man nor do they address the present situation we face individually and as a global village. Homebound chooses titles that balance a reverence for the old sensibilities; while at the same time presenting new perspectives by which to live.

WWW.HOMEBOUNDPUBLICATIONS.COM

CPSIA information can be obtained at www.ICGtesting.com
Printed in the USA
BVOW09s1526060914

365437BV00003B/50/P